THIRD TIME DOWN

THIRD TIME DOWN

Dan Brennan

NEW ENGLISH LIBRARY/TIMES MIRROR

For
Dr. Louis Haselmayer

First published in Great Britain in 1953 by Secker & Warburg Ltd,
under the title of *Time Enough to Live*

© 1961 by Ace Books, Inc.

First NEL Paperback Edition May 1979

NEL Books are published by
New English Library from
Barnard's Inn, Holborn,
London EC1N 2JR
Made and printed in Great Britain by
Hazell Watson & Viney Ltd
Aylesbury, Bucks

45004283 9

CHAPTER ONE

The year I remember it was a late summer. We had a fine mess, a big house in Buckinghamshire just outside of town where we could sit on the lawn and watch the late afternoon fighter patrol coming home line astern through the break in the trees beyond the lawn. There were trees all around the house on the hill, and below on the flats a fighter and a bomber squadron operated. There were Spitfires taking off all day and in the evening we flew out in Whitley bombers to raid Germany and the French coast. There was always talk of an invasion but most of the time we thought the Germans would invade us before we got around to invading them. Yet everybody talked about invading the French coast or a coming secret operation on the coast. It was blinding hot summer and out in the desert the British army was falling back to Cairo and Rommel was on the march.

We had a good time in the evening when we didn't fly. They still had dark Burton ale in the mess though pale ale was rationed. So we sat around and drank Burton's and shot each other a line. Sometimes there was talk about converting to four-engine bombers, but then there were only Stirlings, big stork-legged, heavy-bellied, low altitude four-engine bombers, the first of their kind, and the Aussies were flying them on the squadron which had converted. Sometimes on raids, with the moonlight shining on the clouds below, we saw these four-engine aircraft sailing past in the wave ahead of us. But they were slow for their size and we did not relish changing over from the old two-engine Whitleys.

In the early evening light we could see the Beauforts going out to attack shipping on the Dutch coast. Finally the British held in the desert after many defeats, but there was no feeling of victory to come. It was a long summer with plenty of rain and the hills were green and beautiful all around the airdrome and in the morning when we walked out across the field to our aircraft everything looked more vividly green than ever before.

We had two cars and we cadged high-octane gasoline and somehow kept the two cars operating; usually there were eight to ten of us in each car that held only four according to traffic regulations. We drove into town several times a week if we were not operating. The days were long on double summer time and at midnight the sun was still shining so there were few hours of darkness for raiding. So we raided only France because the night fighters would catch us crossing the Rhine in broad daylight at four in the morning if we penetrated Germany during the summer night hours.

Twice the air marshal of bomber command came to see us, riding in a beautiful gray Bentley. He gave us short pep talks. He said the day was coming when we would be able to attack the Krupp works without having to drop our own flares to find an aiming point. But the Germans were still winning in the desert and in the Atlantic Ocean.

With the fall, when the hours of darkness grew longer, came decisions from bomber command to raid Italy. It was only a gesture to frighten the Italian troops fighting in the African desert. We flew ten hour missions over France and down across the Alps over Mont Blanc, and in three raids on Milan we lost half the squadron. Two tail gunners were carried frozen from their turrets. We did not have electrically heated suits then and the Sidcot suit was not enough against the thirty-below-zero weather above the Alps.

That winter the war stalemated. We heard of a new radar device that would permit us to navigate more easily by sending us a signal from home base so that we could get a direct heading onto the target. It was to be called a G-box. But it did not arrive. Now we were raiding the submarine pens along the French coast and we were out almost every night laying mines off Lorient and St. Nazaire. The Germans were developing a new fighter aircraft but they did not use it, and as a new spring came they began to step up their coastal hit-and-run raids on towns and airfields. Light flak guns were brought into our field and encircled not only the field but the mess, because the Messerschmitts only the day before had strafed a beach and hotel a mile from the field. The air marshal of bomber command came to see us and again talked about

6

the Krupp works and how soon we would be able to attack it, using the new radar navigational device. The war seemed to have steadied down with neither side having a great advantage and you had the feeling that both sides were resting, building up for a great attack.

The next spring I was sent with my crew to Driffield in Yorkshire for a refresher course on fighter tactics, and when I came back there were new machines on our field, fighter bombers, Whirlwinds. Even now in the late summer the fields were green and I thought of home with all the prairie turning brown and the black ground plowed for wheat and corn. Here everything was still green.

The mess had moved. We had a new house and the Whirlwind pilots had our old one. The new mess was a big house, and inside it was cool and the floors were of stone. There was a sergeant sitting at the desk in the hall and I asked him where my room was and he told me I was still billeted with Flight Lieutenant Cuddington. From the window of the bedroom you could see the hills of Buckinghamshire and far away, through the trees, a glint of the Thames taking the sunlight.

The flight lieutenant was sitting in a chair beside the window when I came in. He was reading a map, turning it first one way and then another.

'Well, well,' he said. 'Did you get your master's degree?'

'*Summa cum.*'

He flipped me a pack of Camels.

'How's this?' I asked.

'I have my connections,' he said. 'Please do not inquire into Cuddington's underground. What'd they have you doing up there?'

'The works. Mostly drogue firing for the crew. Fighter co-op. Searchlight battery co-op. Lousy, all of it.'

'You'll be a flight commander before you know it. How was the female situation?'

I looked at him. 'Are you kidding? I didn't meet one girl all the time I was there.'

He rolled his eyes. 'Aha! Then I'm one up on you. I've met a couple of real live dolls. Sisters. Joan and Helene. I must introduce you, but first I must make up my mind which is for you.'

'Fine,' I said and lit one of the Camels. It tasted good after so many months of British cigarettes.

'I'll make up my mind tonight which one you can have,' said Cuddington.

I unpacked my kit bag and he sat at the window studying the map again. He was about twenty-six with black hair and a long lean face. He had been a Canadian bush pilot in the Yukon and Whitehorse territory for almost ten years. He was a fine flier and if he had been younger he would have been on fighters. While I was unpacking he tossed a full pack of American cigarettes on my bed.

'They didn't cost me a dime,' he said. 'Louie's compliments. He's Maltese, some kind of black-market type. I met him in London.'

'Thanks.'

'He's got lots more where these came from, the rat.'

I put my flying boots under the bed. Cuddington, puffing a cigarette, sat there blowing smoke rings, looking out the window now. He said thoughtfully, 'One has gold hair. One has dark hair. It is a great decision. Perhaps I should write home to mother.'

'You're full of it, buster.'

It was a dull evening that night in the mess. There were some new crews, replacements I did not know. I should have been used to it but it was sad, and a little frightening, too, to find old crews gone so quickly. It must be getting rougher over there. I did not think about it because I did not want to and I was able to shut it out in that way. I talked with the adjutant, and, though he was nice, he was dull after a while, and I wished I were driving into London with Cuddington. It was only forty miles but I could see he wanted to go in alone. So I read the evening papers and drank a little too much beer and then went into dinner. There was less meat in the sausages every day now, and the evening reports from the desert fighting were bad.

CHAPTER TWO

In the dawn light I heard the Whirlwind fighter bombers warming up out on the field. Through the veins in the cracked blackout curtain the light beyond was still gray. I turned over on my stomach and listened to the blasting roar of the Rolls-Royce engines, wondering where they were going this morning, excited by the thought, yet glad I was not going out at this hour. Dutch coastal shipping, I thought. I could not sleep with the engines revving, so I lay there listening to them take off, one by one, until the last far faint drone died away upon the morning air. I got up an hour later and went down to the mess and ate breakfast.

After breakfast I walked out to the flight line. It was a beautiful sunny morning. You could see the Whitley bombers, like enormous black bats, with their wings gulled from just beyond the engines to the tips. They squatted in the cement revetments all around the field, dispersed against bombing attacks. The mechanics were working on my plane, W for William. The cowling from the port engine lay on the cement surface under the wing and the mechanics stood on a dolly high against the engine busy with their wrenches.

'When will she be ready?' I asked one of the mechanics.

'Hadley had her out last night. Lost one engine going into the target.' He stood there, his face greasy, his hand busy with the wrench inside the engine.

'Tonight perhaps. She's ropy in the port engine, sir,' he said in a thick Yorkshire accent.

'What's the trouble?'

'An engine change if we had it.'

I walked over to the flight office and went into my locker and hung up my boots and helmet and goggles. I came out past the flight commander's offices and looked out across the field.

Engines were being warmed up, tested, all around the field. The morning was sun-filled, golden-green all around us. I hoped the aircraft would be serviceable; I hoped they would not fail us. You never could tell. Some of the new mechanics were lazy and the old regulars had to keep the aircraft operating by working twelve and thirteen hours a day because spare parts were scarce and we were pounding the old machines. By now we should have new machines, bigger machines, bigger bomb loads, more machine guns, faster-operating power turrets, heavier caliber guns. The German bomber command had lost the Battle of Britain by under-arming their bombers.

I went back to the flight commander's office. He was a big flaxen-haired Scotchman, Jock Shearer, an old fighter pilot transferred to bomber command from the original City of Edinburgh fighter squadron.

'When are we going to get some new planes?' I asked.

He grinned. 'When they get enough of them.'

'Even Wimpey's would be better than these kites.'

'Traitor,' he said.

'I'll be in the mess,' I told him and walked back to the house and read the morning papers I had missed and scrounged a cup of tea from the duty WAAF sergeant in the kitchen. I had never tasted tea like this in America. It was thick, scalding hot, sharp yet sweet with condensed milk. I liked it. It was a great alarm clock. Two cups and you were absolutely wide awake. I sat in the lounge and looked out at the Buckinghamshire hills. It reminded me of the sunny afternoons at home, hunting pheasants across the prairie, the sun high, naked, blinding, hammering heat down upon the wheat fields of Dakota.

That afternoon about four o'clock my plane was ready and I tested it in a brief cross-country flight. The port engine still sounded bad.

The squadron flying personnel seemed to have changed almost completely while I was gone. How long before we could truly attack the Ruhr? I heard rumors of plans to stage a thousand-bomber raid on the Ruhr. It would mean every kite in Britain would be in the air, even training command would have to join in. It would scare the hell out of the Jerries, but, as the squadron leader told me, most of the casualties probably would come from training command because they would send a lot of half-trained crews on the mission to fill out the thousand-bomber plan. The squadron leader said we would be in the first wave.

For the first time they were going to use a wave of pathfinder aircraft to drop flares on the target so we would not have to drop our own flares.

The raid would fall either on some Ruhr Valley target or on a major seaport along the German north coast. Bomber command would send intruder aircraft, Beaufighters, to attack the German night-fighter fields and a single squadron of Blenheims would try a diversionary raid south of the main target to draw off any remaining night fighters. It sounded brilliant on paper but it was a hell of a rough show to travel to in a Whitley. But it would be a smashing success if we pulled it off. For the first time in the history of aerial warfare, a thousand planes would smother the searchlight and flak defenses or at least confuse them after the second wave. It would be something to see.

I went into the bar to get a drink. I was still wearing battle dress. Cuddington was there, drinking Scotch and water. He looked clean and scrubbed and polished in his uniform. He was reading *News of the World*, a Sunday paper.

'Jack,' he said, putting down the newspaper. 'Get yourself slicked up. We've got a date with those dolls in London.'

'Thanks, but I'm going to hit the pad.'

'You need some relaxation.'

'How's the car?'

'Works.'

'Okay,' I said. I did not believe the car could run much longer with the diluted high-octane airplane gas we were putting in it.

I went upstairs, took off my battle dress, shaved, and put on my tunic. We went out to the car behind the mess. The car was an old Lagonda. It was still fast. From under the driver's seat he produced a bottle of Highland Cream.

'Cheers,' Cuddington said. He drank. He handed me the bottle. I drank and the Scotch was fresh and cold and it burned raw going down but in an instant I did not feel so tired.

'Cheers,' I said and drank again and he started the car. It was forty miles to London and we took turns with the Highland Cream all the way in. After the third drink it did not seem to make much difference except the scenery

11

seemed to improve and the usual chimney-cramped roof-tops of outer London took on a certain hazy charm.

We drove along Kensington High Street and Cuddington turned and we stopped in front of one of those narrow, high, gray-stone Kensington houses. Inside it was a beautiful house with good furniture and carpeting. We sat in the living room and two young women came in and Cuddington introduced them. The blonde was Joan DeMarney and the brunette was Helene DeMarney. They did not wear uniforms and I wondered what they were doing in the war because they were certainly old enough to be drafted. But perhaps they were on leave. Despite their French-sounding name they spoke with English accents.

'Are you also Canadian?' Joan asked.

'No. American.'

Cuddington was lighting a cigarette for Helene. She was smiling at him, watching him over the tip of her cigarette. Her eyes and hair were very dark, almost black. It was difficult to believe they were sisters.

'Were you over here when war broke out?' Joan asked.

'No, I came over the usual way. Clayton Knight Committee.'

'What is that?'

'It's in New York. Americans who were in the R.F.C.'

'What do you mean?'

'The old grads sending some new material.'

She looked puzzled.

'What do you do?' I asked. She seemed to pause. 'The war, I mean,' I said.

She looked at me and the lids of her eyes narrowed faintly. Her eyes were very blue, almost violet.

'War office,' she said. Her voice was quite cool, quite level, and there was something in it that said don't ask any more questions. Her eyes seemed to narrow and then widen again.

'Well, are we winning?' I said.

She smiled faintly like someone being solicitous of a schoolboy. Then I saw the ring on her left hand, on the finger of marriage. It was a nice-looking diamond.

'Are you engaged?' I asked.

12

'It was my mother's. She was killed in France.'

'Excuse me.'

'She was with my father. The Germans killed both of them. They took them out and shot them.'

'Were they in the underground?'

She nodded but she did not say anything.

'Is the underground very active now?' I asked.

'I don't know,' she said. 'I don't hear from anybody over there. She gave me the ring before they took her away.'

'How did you escape?'

'Won't you have a drink?'

'We did pretty well in that department driving into town,' I said. She did not move. The expression on her face did not change. She was smoking now and the plume of smoke drifted across her face so I could not see her eyes. She stood there, calmly waiting for me to say something, to change the subject politely or just as politely to accept a drink.

'What do you have?' I asked.

'Sherry. Whiskey.'

'Whiskey,' I said. While she was mixing the drinks from a tray I said, 'I thought you were engaged. You never know what Cuddington's apt to cook up. I suppose he told you once about this attractive girl named Margaret he met who lived in a big house near St. James Park and they had a lot of soldiers guarding it outside when he went to pick her up for a squadron dance and her daddy came out and said—'

Joan began to laugh and lifted her glass. I touched her glass with mine.

'Then you're not engaged?'

'Not at all,' she said.

'Cheers,' I said.

She drank and I drank and we stood there not saying anything after we drank. It had been a long time since I had felt uncomfortable standing with a girl simply because she was beautiful.

'Joan,' I said finally. 'Where would you like to go?'

'I have to get up early.'

'Let's go some place and dance.'

'Ghastly early,' she said. 'Believe me, I must get up.'

'How do you manage to live here?' I asked. I looked

around the room. Maybe she was the head of the war office. General Joan DeMarney, sir.

'My father had the house before the war.'

'Are you French?'

'No, Mother was. Daddy was English.'

'The name sounds—'

'Norman,' she said. She smiled. 'Old, old English invaders.'

Cuddington and Helene were sitting on the davenport across the room. They were laughing and drinking.

'Am I supposed to be with you or her?' I asked.

'Here,' she said, and she reached toward the table and brought the decanter back and poured more whiskey into my glass. Her drink was very light, with just a touch of water in it and as she smoked she seemed only to sip her drink.

'How long have you been over?' she asked.

'Two years.'

'Do you think we'll ever be able to really bomb Germany?'

'You're in the war office, aren't you? Why don't you tell me.'

She looked serious. 'I can't talk about my work. I know how it sounds but I can't. Not even here. We are not supposed to tell. Maybe you might be shot down someday. You do not understand what the Germans will do to people to gain information. I still have a brother in France. I haven't heard from him since last March.

I took a drink.

'Do you like flying?' she asked.

'It's just like the Fourth of July. Lots of Roman candles.'

'What's the Fourth of July?'

'You know Bastille Day? And Guy Fawkes Day? It's all those rolled into one. The day the Americans told their English cousins they were getting a divorce.'

She smiled. 'Oh, Independence Day? George Washington?'

'George,' I said, and touched her glass.

Cuddington called over to us. 'Hey, Jack, let's get these girls on their feet and shake a leg.'

'We can't,' Helene said.

Cuddington slapped his hand against the side of his head.

He looked at me. 'How about that?' he said. 'Forty miles. Jack, didn't I tell you they were a couple of lovely dolls?' He shook his head with exaggerated regret. 'A couple of girl guides, it looks like.'

'Any other night,' Helene said. 'We have to be at work early.'

'Darling,' Cuddington said. 'I go to work late. Midnight. I get home early. Tonight I'm willing to stay up for you.'

Helene put her hand on his shoulder and looked at her sister.

'Really,' she said. 'We have to sleep tonight. We have to start at five tomorrow.'

Cuddington shrugged. 'Shot down over base,' he said. 'Come on, Jack.' He looked at his watch. He kissed Helene's cheek and she laughed and pushed him away. I had the feeling he had not done it before and he was doing it for my benefit but you could never tell about Cuddington. I had seen him on some strange and successful romantic campaigns.

I finished my drink and stood up.

'Good night,' I said. 'Thank you for the drink.' We went outside and drove down to Shepherd's Bar in Shepherd Market. There was a gang in there from the fighter squadron at Biggin Hill Airfield. We stood at the bar and Cuddington said, 'How about that? Forty miles. Those dolls said they would be home.'

'Where did you meet them?'

'They were in here with a couple of British colonels. A slight beam attack, firing all of Cuddington's charm and—'

'You looked real good, brother. Remind me to send regrets next time.'

'Collations?' he said.

'Libation,' I said.

'Bartender,' Cuddington said. 'Two dark brown ales, please.'

CHAPTER THREE

I thought about Joan the next morning. In fact, I thought about her that night driving back to the field. I phoned the war office late the next afternoon. Nobody knew of her. I called the house. Her sister answered the telephone. Helene said they did not like the girls to be called at the war office so they simply told callers they were not known and that stopped the calls.

'I want to get hold of her tonight,' I said.

'She's busy.' There was a long pause. The wire sounded as if it were dead. Then Helene's voice: 'I'll be home about six.'

'I'll tell Paul.'

She started to say something else and stopped.

'Tell her I called. I'll call back.'

'I'm sure she's busy.'

Paul, my boy, I thought, this is a real night fighter, this Helene; you'll have to close to point-blank range or disengage attack.

'Tell her I'll be in town,' I said. 'About seven.'

'All right.'

'Thank you,' I said and hung up. She had not looked the type. I would have to tell Paul to keep his hands up. This Helene was quite a little infighter. Maybe Paul needed a little infighting. Maybe the boy was going stale.

I went over to the mess and washed and changed clothes and got the car and drove into London. Kensington was a beautiful part of London.

'I rang the doorbell at Joan's house and Helene opened the door. Beside her was a tall Australian squadron leader. He wore a big sandy-red cavalry mustache.

'We're just going out,' Helene said. 'Peter, this is—' She paused, gave me an acid-sweet smile. 'Oh, I'm sorry. I've forgotten your name.'

'Jack,' I said. 'Jack O'Hara.' I looked at my watch.

'Oh, of course,' Helene said with the same acid-sweet smile and introduced us. Then she turned her head back into the hall and called Joan.

I was standing in the hall when Joan came down.

'Oh, it's you,' she said, surprised. She paused at the foot of the stairs.

'Didn't Helene tell you I called?'

'She didn't say anything to me.'

'How about dinner?'

'Well, uh—' she began.

I looked at my watch.

'Come on.' I took her arm, held her elbow in one hand. 'Get your coat. I've got the car.'

'Isn't gasoline rationed?'

'Official business,' I said.

'All right,' she said. She went back upstairs. She returned wearing a coat. We went outside and got in the car.

'Where would you like to eat?'

'I don't care,' she said.

'What do you do at the war office? Do you really work there?'

She smiled. It was getting dark outside now. In a few minutes it would be dark. The light was coming green in deep twilight through the trees. I drove down to Hyde Park Corner and along Piccadilly until we came to Half-Moon Street. I parked and we went into the Lansdowne Club and got a table near the orchestra.

I asked her again about the war office.

'I file papers.'

The band began to play. I asked her to dance and we stood up and went out onto the floor. She was a beautiful dancer. The lights went down and I held her close in the darkness. She did not move away. We danced on around the floor. I kissed her cheek and she drew back her head.

'No thanks,' she said, holding her face back and away.

'Is there someone else?' I asked.

'Not at all. Just don't do it again, please.'

'I probably will.'

'I rather doubt it.'

'Don't be too sure.'

I had played this game with a lot of women. I could wait. It would take time, that was all.

The lights came on and we sat down and the waiter came and we ordered. She asked for gin and dubonnet and I ordered whiskey and water.

'You're very attractive,' I said.

'I know,' she said. 'And you always kiss the attractive ones.'

'Right.'

'Tomorrow we die. I suppose that's next.'

'That's strictly a last resort.'

'You're pleasant without working at it so hard,' she said.

We talked about the war and we danced and ate dinner. The band stopped playing early and we went out to the car. Faraway upon the night air the guns were firing, some place down along the river. It was a moonlit night and the searchlights were working the sky.

I opened the car door for her and she got in and I went around the other side and got in and leaned over and put my arm around her and kissed her. I kissed her lips but she did not return the kiss. I tried to draw her close but she pulled away. I thought, to hell with it, and then suddenly she put her arms around me and kissed me, and she was saying something in my ear but her voice was so low I could not hear and I whispered, 'What?'

She said, 'Hold me, Jack. Hold me close.' Her voice was tense. What's this? I thought. I kissed her again and her lips were soft and gentle and I could feel her body tremble against me as with a chill.

'Oh, God, don't,' she said. 'You don't understand.' She pulled away. 'I'm a fool.'

I drove her back to Kensington and kissed her at the door but she stopped everything again. I drove back to the field and went into the mess. To hell with her. The bar was full. Half the squadron were just back from a raid on Lille. Cuddington was standing at the bar with a grease stain on his cheek. He turned and held up his glass of beer.

'Join me,' he said. He signaled the bartender. 'I damn near bought it tonight.'

'What happened?'

'Stupid navigator said we were clear of the French coast. I held it straight and level a few minutes and all hell broke loose. Big blue light had us conned and they put predicted flak on us. That poor kite really got a ringing out.'

The beer came.

'Cheers,' he said, and drank the pint fast. I stood there wondering about Joan.

18

The next two nights we flew on short raids to the Dutch coast. The third night of that week the squadron stood down. I phoned Joan. She told me not to come to the house. She would meet me at Shepherd's Bar. I waited in the bar sitting in one of the corner chairs. They were big overstuffed chairs and strange to find in a bar at that time. It was a nice bar and you could eat upstairs. It was always full of uniforms from all the services but mostly from the RAF.

I sat in the corner and relaxed. I was tired and ordered a beer. I thought about the rest of my tour. About ten more missions and I would be screened, taken off combat, and sent to teach new pilots at an operational training unit. This would be my second tour of ops. The odds were increasing. I told myself to stop thinking about it. It was bad if you thought about it. Nerves. It was a sure sign if you started figuring the odds. Either you'd had it or you hadn't. Odds didn't mean anything.

I didn't see Joan DeMarney until she called my name and then I turned and saw her. She was standing almost beside my chair and I stood up. She was the best-looking woman in the room.

'Hello, Jack,' she said.

The waiter was standing there already.

'Hello,' I said. 'What will you have?'

'Sherry,' she said. I drew up a chair and she sat down and the waiter went away.

'Would you like to eat here?' I asked.

'I'm really not very hungry,' she said. Somehow her eyes looked different, strained, tense. The waiter returned with her drink and when she had finished it she said, 'Let's go for a ride.'

'Sure,' I said. 'We can eat later.'

We went out to the car and tooled along Curzon Street.

'I thought you were dead,' she said suddenly.

'It's only a rumor.'

'I phoned twice,' she said. She sounded quite serious.

'When?'

'Yesterday afternoon and the day before. They wouldn't put me through to you and whoever answered wouldn't give me any information when I might reach you.'

'We were on ops,' I said. 'We can't take any phone calls after briefing.'

'I thought surely you'd been shot down and they were trying to be nice and cover up.'

I turned off Park Lane and drove down to Berkeley Square and stopped the car. I put my arm around her and kissed her.

'Let's go in the park,' I said.

'I was sure you were dead,' she said.

'Not yet.'

'Why do you take me out?' she asked.

I didn't say anything.

'I know,' she said.

'I'm fond of you,' I said, thinking. Oh, my God, does it always end this way? To make love to them, to the nice ones, do you have to tell them you love them? I wasn't going to get involved with all the lies she wanted to hear simply because she wanted to feel like a nice girl. It wasn't worth it. It would only lead to complications and some kind of social consequences. I couldn't cope with that kind of business now.

'Fond of me?' she said and laughed softly. 'Oh, really, you talk a lot of rubbish.'

I kissed her again to stop her talking and to stop myself from giving her any more lies.

After a while I took my arm away and we sat in the car and looked up at the moon through the leafy branches of the trees. It was a fine night for night fighters, a nice big round moon and no cloud. I was very happy to be here in Berkeley Square. You're getting too jumpy, I thought. Maybe this was a bad thing. Maybe I ought to pack it up before it got too late. There were all kinds of girls around. You could always find a girl.

'Do you have many missions to do yet?' she asked.

'About ten.'

She sat motionless, making no sound, for a long moment.

'You just want to play around, don't you?'

'No,' I said. 'Of course not.'

'Rubbish.'

'All right. Sure,' I said.

'I should know better.'

'Don't ask then.'

20

'I know what you want. I knew from the beginning.'

'I said I was fond of you.'

'Don't work so hard at it, Jack.'

'Forget it.' I started the engine. She suddenly caught my hand. I turned and looked at her. To hell with it, I thought. 'Would it be better if I told you I loved you? Is that what you want to hear?' I said.

'You don't have to say anything.'

'I love you, Joan.'

'Bravo.'

I shifted gears and turned out of the square and drove her home.

She got out of the car, opening the door herself on her side and I started to get out.

'Don't come up,' she said. 'Good night, Jack.'

I walked around the car. She was already going up the steps. I caught up to her and touched her shoulder and turned her around and kissed her.

She drew her mouth away. She did not look at me.

'Good night, Jack,' she said, and I watched her open the door and go inside. She was a very beautiful girl.

CHAPTER FOUR

Two days later we heard the attack was to be laid on Cologne some night that week. I got the car and drove into London. I did not want to phone Joan first, I had the feeling she might put me off if I did. I parked down the block from the house and walked up and rang the doorbell. Helene came to the door.

'Is Joan in?'

'She's busy.'

'Come on,' I said. 'Call her.'

She wrinkled her nose, made a face, and went upstairs. A few minutes later Joan came down.

'I didn't know you wore glasses.'

'Only when I'm working.'

'Are you busy?'

'I can't go out, if that's what you mean,' she said.

'I hoped you could make it tonight.'

21

'Why didn't you phone?'

Just then Helene put her head over the banister and told me I was wanted on the telephone. The phone was on a stand at the end of the hall. Who knew where I was? It was Cuddington.

'Hey, boy, that you?'

'Receiving.'

'Get your fanny back,' he said.

'What's up?'

'A big party.' His voice sounded different.

'I thought the party was later. Tomorrow.'

'Tonight. We're inviting everybody.'

'Right,' I said and hung up and turned to Joan.

'I've got to go.'

'What's the matter?'

'That was Paul. They're laying on a big attack tonight.'

'I know. I heard this afternoon. But they called it off.'

'It's on again,' I said.

'Kiss me, Jack,' she said.

She put her arms around my neck. I kissed her a long time and held her tight. She seemed suddenly quite small. My mouth was dry.

'Be careful,' she said.

'I'll put my hand out on every turn.'

'It sounds silly, I know.'

'Take care of yourself,' I said and kissed her again. She held her arms around my shoulders. Her hands were cold.

'I've got to go,' I said.

'Good luck,' she said. I walked straight down the hall and out the front door and opened it and closed it without looking back at her.

I drove fast back to the field. The crews were walking from their quarters to the big Nissen hut used for briefing before an attack. They walked in pairs, carrying thermos flasks. I went down to my room and changed clothes and went up to the briefing. There were two officers in the room from the Royal Artillery. One of them wore air gunner wings. They were going along on the raid to study the German flak.

On the map of Europe on the wall at the end of the room the colored ribbons marked the routes of the attacking force. There was to be a diversionary attack both in northern Germany and southern Germany. I saw the blue ribbon stretching across the map to Frankfurt and a green ribbon in the north stretching across to Emden. They would use fast fighter-bombers in these attacks.

I sat there and listened to the weather reports. Broken cloud over the target but generally clear and no icing below twenty-two thousand. There were more than a thousand heavy flak guns defending the target and three bands of searchlights. We would turn down from the north after crossing the Zuider Zee and run out over the target from the south. I did not like this but it was the only way out. A slight mistake in navigation would take us directly over all the flak defenses of the Ruhr on the way home. We could easily run into Essen, Cologne, Düsseldorf, for all of these cities lay in a cluster along the river.

It was almost dark when we came out of briefing.

Now, as on many nights before, I looked out of the cockpit and watched the moving tip of my port wing. I could feel the bomber rearing big on the tires, rolling, turning onto the flare path. I checked the gunner in the tail turret and watched the control tower for a green flare. I could feel my heart beating fast, and a quick gust of loneliness. Looking out into the fading dusk I watched the crowd on the grass alongside the flare path, a clotting of dark figures, a few hands raised in thumbs up, ground crew and others waving good-bye. A green flare burst like a monstrous match against the gathering darkness.

I held the brakes down hard and gunned the engines. The fuselage shuddered all along its frame. I snapped off the brakes. The grass trembled, flattened on each side of the flare path. Then we were moving and I could feel the engines gathering power and a cold sweat in the palm of one hand. I pushed the control wheel forward and felt the tail rise and watched the air speed increase and suddenly we were airborne. The treetops fled past. Figures on the ground dissolved, swallowed into darkness.

We climbed steadily and up here above the darkness you could see the dying sunlight still bright in the sky. Remote as a gull we climbed slowly into the empty evening sky. I squeezed a few raisins into my mouth, under the oxygen mask.

'Hello, Steve,' I said. 'How about a course to the coast?'
'Half a mo, Jack.'
Steve was a Canadian from Edmonton.
'Okay, Jack,' he said. 'Steer one-eight-six magnetic.'
'Have you got an E.T.A. to the coast yet?'
'Half a mo.'
'Turning on course . . . on course, Steve.'
'Righto, boy.'
The sky was rosy, golden, washed in a sea of evening light. Other bombers, black as bats, hovered motionless all around us, setting course.

We began to climb steadily, and looking down I could see the earth going farther and farther away. There were a few clouds below, and through a break I saw the Thames, twisting and shining like a long silver snake.

'E.T.A. to the coast, Jack, is seventeen fifty-two,' Steve said. 'About twenty minutes.'

I saw the sun was almost gone, and high overhead daylight faded and the darkness rising from the ground came up slowly like a fast sea of darkening water. I talked with the crew. The tail gunner had his guns checked and cocked, ready to fire. I asked the radio operator if the loop antenna was functioning properly and he called up with a loop bearing within a few minutes.

The bombardier came up from the nose turret and poured two cups of tea from his thermos and handed me one. It was pitch dark outside now. I drank the tea with my oxygen mask unhooked and hoped my kidneys would hold all right until after we came off the target. I asked Steve for another fix and then told the crew we were approaching the Dutch coast and in five minutes we would begin to take evasive action and to watch for night fighters.

'There's some new fighters with green and red lights,' the rear gunner said. 'I'll call the position of the green light first and you turn into that.'

'Have I got time to go to the can?' the bombardier asked.

'You ought to work from there, Al,' somebody said.

'Turn it off,' I said. 'Keep your eyes peeled for night fighters.'

I began to take evasive action, doing slow long half-turns both starboard and port. It was standard procedure. I did not believe it helped because a flak battery could predict you on a mean course, and the only way to throw off their predictor lay in a change of altitude; but now we needed all the altitude we could get so we could put the nose down after bombing and come home flat out, full speed.

It was dark below coming up to the Dutch coast and then the long beams of the searchlights south of us sabered the sky suddenly and began moving and probing. There was a big long blue searchlight at Amsterdam that you had to be careful to miss if you were running in between Rotterdam and Amsterdam.

You couldn't dive out of this light. It had the longest beam in Europe. I had never seen another like it. We crossed the coast on time and changed course and headed north. A slice of the moon was shining now, and in the dark the light shone down upon the Zuider Zee. Far-away to the north flak burst, green and red and yellow, in great sparkling showers, hanging briefly in the sky. They were firing chandelier flares to silhouette the pathfinders. It reminded me of Fourth of July night at the amusement park back home. It was very beautiful at a distance. The radio operator called on the intercom.

'Message from base,' he said. 'We're being followed by night fighters.'

I looked ahead in the darkness. The sky was black and empty. Far ahead a few searchlights were moving. Suddenly dead ahead I saw the first yellow flare falling through the sky, marking our turning point north of the target. Then another yellow flare, then a cluster, then the sky was suddenly webbed with searchlight beams and the flak defenses began firing.

'Weave!' the tail gunner yelled. 'Weave, Jack! They're trying to get a light on us.'

I dived starboard and then climbed.

'What's E.T.A. to target?' I asked.

'Ten minutes. Bang on,' said Steve.

Flak burst now at regular intervals on each side of the plane, a long string of round black balls of smoke with an orange flash in the center. I could hear the shrapnel falling like buckshot against the fuselage.

'Steer two-five-oh,' Steve said. 'We're turning on.'

25

A loud burst of flak exploded close and again I could hear the shrapnel raining down on the metal fuselage.

Then I saw the first target markers falling through the forest of searchlight beams ahead. Red flare on red flare fell into the lights, and suddenly there was a glare and sparkle on the ground. The first fire bombs were on target.

I checked the altimeter, pushed the nose down faintly. We were going to run in now on the target. I looked for a hole in the mass of searchlight beams. There was none. Cone after cone of searchlights surrounded the target. I waited for another aircraft to fall into the cone. I could see the minute white puffs of shell fire bursting around him. A string of black balls burst straight ahead in a flash of orange fire. Then I heard a loud explosion directly under the bomber and felt the controls buck. I kicked on the top rudder. The tail gunner was shouting to weave. The sky was filled with round black balls of shell fire. A plane hurtled past with flames streaming back like pennants from one engine.

'Here we go,' I said.

'Left a little, Jack,' Steve said.

I eased the wheel over.

'Hold her, Jack. Hold her!'

My mouth felt dry and my guts cold. I looked out at the shell fire and searchlights. The sky was crazy with color – flares, lights, burning machines falling, searchlights weaving.

An explosion shook the bomber again.

'Rockets,' somebody said. 'They're using rockets.'

I checked the air-speed indicator and took a deep gulp of oxygen. I stared down into the darkness, the bowl of light that marked the target.

'Fighters!' a voice yelled over the intercom. Ahead I saw a green light flashing, apparently suspended in mid-air. My guts coiled. Christ, fighters signaling each other!

'Turn starboard!' the tail gunner yelled. 'Turn starboard!'

I kicked the rudder. The machine seemed to take a century to come out of the dive. It was skidding. Damn it, were we turning tight enough into the attack?

The darkness overhead was filled with blue flashes. I felt the machine buck under the impact of cannon fire.

'Call out the fighter!' I said to the tail gunner. 'Where is the bastard?'

Dead ahead the thin black line of the night fighter's wing flashed bluely. Long threads of tracer fire whizzed past. Glass burst in my face and I felt cold air rush in. A hot, shocking explosion struck me suddenly in the shoulder and leg.

'Oh, my God,' I heard a voice moaning on the intercom. 'Oh, my God, I'm hit!'

'Turn port! Turn port!' the tail gunner yelled. 'Here comes another!' I could hear his machine guns firing.

My legs and hands felt as if they were burning. Again the darkness was filled with blue flashes, cannon fire from the night fighter. I felt liquid running down the side of my face. The glass in front of my face was shot away. I pulled back on the wheel and the machine continued to dive. I heard myself scream suddenly with pain. My hands and legs were on fire. I slapped at my legs with both hands. My leather gloves were on fire. I slapped again at my legs.

'Bail out!' I yelled. 'Bail out!' I grabbed the wheel again. The plane pulled up, stalled, and I saw the stars wheel. Flak burst like sheet lightning all around us and I heard the explosion of more cannon shells along the fuselage. It all happened in a few seconds. Then the sky swung. Oh, Christ, I was burning alive. The oxygen was on fire. Christ, I would fry.

'Bail out!' I screamed. 'Bail out!' The wheel slipped from my hands and I flung off my gloves. I smelled my flesh burning and I saw flames coming from my leather flying boots. I lashed out with both legs, trying to kick the boots free. I tried to grab the wheel again to keep it from stalling but it was too late and for a second the bomber stood straight up on its nose and then we were falling somewhere over Holland.

I saw my hands scrabbling to free my body from the Sutton harness but when I was free I could not move. I felt pressure hammering me down into the seat and knew I was in a steep dive. It would only be a few seconds and the wing would pull off. I looked at the air-speed indicator. We were doing close to three hundred. I tried to rise but could not move. My legs burned. I pushed down with both hands but still could not move. The darkness rushed upward, whirling, filled with red-and-white flashes.

I got hold of the control wheel, got both feet braced in an agony of pain against the instrument panel and pulled. I felt my arms pulling in the shoulder sockets but the wheel would not move. I pulled again. I could not breathe. I pulled again and again. Liquid ran into one eye. I could see only faintly, and then slowly, I could hear my mind saying into the panting, into the breathlessness, *Come on, come on*. I began to curse and then gradually, so gradually, I felt the wheel come back. I screamed. I pulled at the wheel. The flesh was almost burned off one hand. I felt the flesh move on my hand and then the starlight came level. A burst of light flak wound slowly upward. God, I thought, I'll never make it. I'll never make it. I felt crazy with pain. I looked at the compass. It had stopped spinning and the altimeter showed two thousand feet. I looked out at the stars and swung the wheel hard over on a dead-reckoning course for England.

CHAPTER FIVE

The moon was brilliant. I could see clouds above like layers of whipped cream. I could hold the wheel with one hand but every second I felt my breath going away and I felt myself fainting. The fire in the port engine was out. The dive must have killed it, but the prop was windmilling. The machine floundered along like a stricken animal. I kept shaking my head to keep myself from passing out. Every second was agony. I mustn't pass out, I told myself. I mustn't. Then I passed out.

You hear stories of how men get themselves free of a plane without knowing how. Well I do not know how I got free of my plane, but when I became conscious I was falling rapidly. I pulled the ripcord of my parachute and felt the upward jerk as the 'chute checked my descent.

I looked down and in the moonlight I saw my trousers were burned off above the knees. I could see nothing below in the darkness. I did not know where I was. Then suddenly I saw water below. I struggled to undo my parachute but I failed and struck the sea with the 'chute falling over me. Later, in the hospital, I decided the plane must have turned over on its back and I was thrown out.

I came up out of the water and realized I was floating and the water was not cold. I'm somewhere in the channel near shore, I thought. Then I smelled myself, the burned flesh, and I felt sick. I lay back in the sea and floated. How long would it take to die? The water grew colder but my Mae West kept me floating. My teeth began to chatter with cold.

I was horrified by the image of dying like this but I was no longer afraid. You'll know soon, I thought. It won't be long. An hour. Two hours. I lay there thinking of the squadron coming home to the mess, and of Joan. I had been brought up to pray. but I felt no desire now to pray. I felt very lonely.

It was dark for a long time and I became colder. Somewhere I heard a whistle and I thought perhaps I was going insane. I began to laugh and I heard the whistle blowing again. Then I saw a faint light upon the water. I tried to discern the shape of the light as it vanished. Then again, somewhere behind me, the whistle trilled shrilly, two cold thin blasts across the chill darkness. I should have known then what it was for one hung from my battlejacket collar.

Then across the water the solitary dot of light appeared to search for me in the dark. 'Hello!' I shouted. 'Hello!' My voice sounded small against the cold spray blowing now from the water.

The dot of light vanished. I tried to paddle toward it but the cold water pained my hands. I lay back, turning my head to one side, facing the direction from which the light had come. I floated, listening and peering across the dark water. Twice the whistle trilled, meaningless, lost. High overhead, above the thin mist, came the sound of engines, passing, dying away.

I fell asleep, though I tried not to sleep, and I slept thinking I was dead, so that when the hand touched me the feeling of being carried, suspended, meant nothing to me. Only a dream. I was sure I was dead. I had not intended to sleep, but in the dark I heard voices. The hands ceased touching me, and I woke completely.

It was still dark and there was the sound of the sea all

29

around the dinghy in which I lay; the dinghy climbed the crest of a wave, dropped down the opposite side. I tried to sit up, fell back. Opposite, on the floor of the dinghy, lay a young man. Another young man sat beside him, looking down. Behind the seated young man, three more young men crouched, huddled. The young man on the dinghy floor was covered with Irving flying jackets, the top of his head wrapped in white wool flying sweaters. No one spoke.

High over head the night flight of bombers passed on and on across the sky, the snarl of their engines fading away. Then the wind began to blow, biting the tips off the waves, thinning the icy water to sharp spray. The dinghy lay for an instant in a trough between two waves, then scooted upward atop a wave. The men grasped the sides of the dinghy. Caught off balance and weak, I almost fell out. One of the men caught my leg.

As the dinghy reached the top of the wave, the three young men clutched the shoulders of the prone young man and held him down to keep him from being thrown out. But the prone young man did not move. He lay motionless, his face a death mask. The dinghy began to fill with water, sliding down the opposite side of the wave. Between the next two waves, they released the prone young man. He groaned and muttered. I watched them. They bailed water furiously with their bare hands. I felt terrible pain now that my flesh was cold.

When the moon appeared through a rift in the clouds, I saw the four figures in battle dress. They sat like rigid, wooden idols, cross legged behind the prone man. One was a pilot officer. In random glints, moonlight caught the metal flight-sergeant crowns on the sleeves of the three young men seated alongside the pilot officer. Across the water, the sea distances stretched away into the darkness.

'Where are we?' I asked. The officer shook his head. Clouds slid over the moon.

'Thanks for fishing me out,' I said. Still the pilot officer said nothing. He only nodded his head as if he were saving his energy or trying to fight off sleep.

'I thought I'd had it,' I said. The sergeants and the officer stared at me. They smiled faintly.

Suddenly, far away, heavy as thunder, gunfire rumbled across the sky. The wind began to die and the waves subsided. The prone flier did not stir. After a few minutes the wind began to rise. The prone flier moved, turning slightly under the piled Irving jackets. He mumbled, 'Alice . . . Alice . . .' He groaned and stirred a little more.

I saw the pilot officer bend over the young man. 'No, Harry.' His voice was quiet and gentle. 'Everything's fine, Harry.' The officer stooped his head again, his face close to the prone young flier.

'Hell,' said one of the sergeants to the officer. 'He'll never make it. Let's—'

The officer turned his head, his glare hard and cold. 'Shut up, Cox.'

The dinghy rolled and tossed from wave to wave. The group huddled silently. The moon shone briefly again, revealing only the rough, dark water. Somewhere in the distance, coastal guns were firing; overhead another wave of invisible bombers passed and died away.

I stared up into the darkness. The other men looked up at the invisible sound, their faces gaunt, almost abject, yet with a strange ferocity.

'Lucky bastards,' said one sergeant.

'Save your breath, Al,' the officer said, following the sound overhead with his gaze. 'We can't be very far out. They'll find us in the morning.' He continued looking upward, waiting for a rift in the clouds.

'You won't get a fix off any stars tonight,' the sergeant said. Again the sound of the sea, a vast silence, enveloped us, while we rocked punily under the sky.

'How long have you been out?' I asked.

'Two days.' The officer's voice ceased. Again the sea calmed. A fine, even spray blew across the air; the clouds parted and moonlight glinted on the spray until it resembled sparks of ice. Again the wind blew strongly.

Suddenly one sergeant tapped the officer on the shoulder and then lifted his arm. He pointed toward something invisible in the darkness. The sergeant slanted his head and shouted at the officer. The officer shook his head. Above the rising wind I could not hear their voices. Again the sergeant pointed. We turned our heads and squinted into the darkness. It was impenetrable. 'Light!' the sergeant shouted. He cupped his hands around his lips. 'Can't you see it?'

31

I could not see anything. Only thick darkness. Again the clouds left the sea moonless. The dinghy mounted the crest of another wave. The officer sat silent. As the dinghy slid down the wave the sergeant shouted again and pointed. 'There it is! Over there!' His voice was high and thin, quite shrill now. He waved his arm wildly. A dark wave rose ahead. Everybody gripped the sides of the dinghy. We huddled and waited silently.

The sea and the sky and the darkness enclosed us after a long while in a windless silence, as tranquil, lost and empty as the face of the moon. The dinghy rested almost motionless upon the water. The sky arched quiet and still dark.

Suddenly the officer stood up and peered forward. 'What's that?'

We rose to our knees, staring blindly into the water.

'There!' the officer cried. 'A ship!' He pointed again. I could see nothing.

Then it appeared, its slightly jagged crest of funnel and radio mast looming in the distance. Standing, the officer blew the whistle attached to the collar of his jacket. Three short, even blasts that left only a following isolated silence in which there was no answer. Then, in silhouette, the lines of the ship resolved, slowly as a photo negative in developing solution, bow, stern and gunwhale. A silence hung on the air, as if emanating from the ship; it appeared motionless, seen in stark relief against a lighting sky.

Then the dinghy bumped alongside the ship. Something rough and coarse touched my hand; a rope. My hand shaped to it, and I grasped it and screamed with pain.

'A lift here, lads,' the officer said, and two sergeants carried me up against the side of the trawler and lifted me aboard. The prone young man was already on deck. He began to cry and moan. I looked down at him.

The others climbed aboard, bringing the Irving jackets and the flying sweaters. They covered the wounded man, then stood looking about, their faces sober and relieved.

'Hello!' the officer shouted. There was no answer. Only the water slapping against the sides of the trawler.

Sergeant Cox moved over close to the officer. 'What do you make of it, sir?'

'I don't know,' the officer said. 'We'd better have a look around.'

I could walk and the cold air was agony upon my hand so I went on toward the cabin with the officer and the sergeant. The others remained behind, squatting about the wounded man. Wan, cold light was appearing, a thin streak in the sky.

The officer drew his breath across his teeth. 'What's this?'

The officer and I halted.

The door of the cabin was partly bashed in, punctured at random with bullet holes. Cox kicked the door aside and looked in. The room was filled with gray, pallid light, the color of water. Upon the floor, among broken and overturned tables and chairs, amid the circular red stain that had only recently ceased to widen, sprawled upon their backs and faces, were six bodies, three in fishermen's rubber mackintoshes, three in soft leather Luftwaffe flying suits. Two Luger pistols lay beside the bodies. On the floor beside one fisherman's head lay the smashed, tangled mass of a broken radio and telegraph key: killed in a struggle over the radio after they had rescued the Germans from the sea. We turned and went outside.

Already daylight was more than a rumor. 'Al,' the officer called. 'Have a look astern. See if there's anything to eat.'

We returned to the group huddled around the wounded man. A wind was rising, only slight, but the trawler began to roll. The sergeant returned with a tin of sodden crackers.

'Nothing else,' he said.

'A treasure,' the officer said and passed the crackers around. The wounded man opened his eyes. The officer gave him a cracker to suck on. He smiled faintly, childlike, and nibbled at the cracker.

On the eastern horizon a faint streak of light widened slowly, drawing the pallid grayness out of the air; the trawler began to roll steadily. The sun appeared; the men looked at each other. Then it was daylight and we looked out across the sea.

A few hours later a dot appeared on the horizon. The pain was bad now that I was thawing out. I wanted to

33

scream. God, if only they had a hypo. I chewed my lips, felt salty liquid like stale copper pennies in my mouth.

Suddenly everybody began to wave and jump up and down. Somebody laughed and shouted. Presently the dot materialized – a launch. Oh, God, get me a hypo, I thought, get it quick, before I scream. I can't stand much more of this. I looked over at the wounded man, tried to let my mind wander but it would not wander. It was sensitive only to pain. The wounded man had closed his eyes, the sodden biscuit lay half-eaten in one outstretched slack hand. A man in the bow of the launch waved. I could see him smiling. Then the launch was alongside.

'Give us a stretcher,' the officer called across.

One of the men laughed. Then Sergeant Cox bent over the wounded man. Below his gaze the wounded man's face lay hushed and smooth, the eyes closed, the patient lips turned down at the corners.

There were three first-aid men aboard. I closed my eyes, waited gratefully for the needle. I could not stop the sensation of falling. It was horrible. I opened my eyes. I was lying on a bunk.

'We got hit just inside the Dutch coast,' I said. 'The others bailed out. For God's sake, give me a shot of something. My hands are killing me.'

'Take it easy, Mack. The M.O. will fix you up in a jiffy.'

I waited and waited and I knew I couldn't take the pain much longer. I wanted to faint but could not.

'Come on,' I said. 'Come on. Give me a hypo.'

We docked at Yarmouth. There was an ambulance waiting but now the pain was hooded and I felt a sense of luxuriant relaxation. I'm out of it, I thought. I won't have to go back. I'm out of it. I had not been scared like this before, and as I thought these thoughts I felt ashamed and afraid and cowardly, yet glad I was out of it. We drove a long way, and when they opened the back curtains of the ambulance a station orderly with a Polish insignia on his shoulder lifted me out on the stretcher.

'Where are we?' I asked.

'Catfoss,' somebody said. They carried me into the sick bay and put me on the floor. There were no medical personnel around until an RAF doctor came in. He knelt down and with a pair of scissors began to cut away my trousers and jacket.

'You're lucky,' he said.

'Real lucky,' I said. He went on cutting and a medical orderly knelt down and began taking dictation from the doctor. He was telling him about my burns.

An intelligence officer entered, knelt down. 'Was it fighters or flak?'

I longed to sleep. 'Both,' I said.

'What got you?'

'Fighters finally. I'm thirsty as hell.'

'Sergeant,' the doctor called, 'bring him a cup of tea. Hot. Quick.'

I did not look up. I felt him sprinkling powder on my legs.

The doctor said, 'Shock. Get him over to the hospital.'

They wrapped me in a blanket.

'Where's the tea?' I did not really care but I could feel myself slipping away and I was afraid suddenly to sleep. I was afraid of something more than sleep. I felt cold and began to shake again. They laid more blankets over me. That was all I remembered until I woke up in the hospital and the doctor leaning over me turned out to be from the Mayo Clinic. When I told him where my home town was, he said, 'You won't die. Nobody dies from North Dakota.'

He was very hearty and jolly about it all. I tried to sound interested but I did not care. I felt sick. I waited a long time, afraid to close my eyes because the falling sensation came. Then I passed out and in a dream I saw Cuddington's plane on fire, the engines jerking flames in the searchlights. Then in the dream I felt bugs running over my hands and legs.

CHAPTER SIX

The fire was crawling up my legs. I could not get out of the fire. The oxygen bottle had burst and I was being fried. I could hear myself screaming. I was filled with terror. Oh, God, if only I could bail out. If only I could bail out. I felt

35

sick with the smell of my flesh burning. Then I was falling clear. The air was cool and I woke. There was no pain.

I saw the walls of the hospital room and the face of a woman in the nurse's uniform in front of me. Then I became aware of my hands and legs. They felt heavy and stiff.

'Don't move,' she said. 'Don't move at all.'

I looked down at my hands. They looked brown and claw-like, curled on the sheet in front of me.

'What is it?' I asked.

'Tannic acid. They've scrubbed and sprayed your hands.'

'What hospital is it?'

She told me the name but I can't even remember it now. It was some place in Kent.

'Lie very still,' she said.

'Good Lord, I'm thirsty,' I said. 'May I have a beer?'

'Ginger beer.'

'Anything.'

She went out and I lay there and wondered why my hands and legs did not hurt. There was no pain. Then I moved my head and my vision blurred and the room swung and an immense lassitude seized me and I knew, thank God, they were keeping me under morphine. After I drank the ginger beer I felt violently hungry. I rang for the nurse.

'I'd like some dinner or breakfast or whatever time it is,' I said. The shades were drawn.

'You can't eat yet,' she said.

'I'm starving.'

She was a big fat woman and she laughed and her chin wattles jiggled.

'I know how you feel, but you can't eat.'

'When can I?'

'Maybe tomorrow. Or the day after.' She went out.

I fell asleep. I dreamed I was over Mont Blanc. We were flying to raid Turin. The moon hung high and naked, shining down on the snowy peak. A flare was on fire in the plane. It was stuck in the chute. It would not fall out and somebody was screaming at me on the intercom, asking if he should bail out. I woke soaked with sweat and shaking. They were changing my dressings. There were two nurses in the room.

Two days later I had my first solid meal. But after eating I felt only a complete sense of apathy.

The days went on after that, changing dressings, sleeping, dreaming, feeling weak one moment and excited and strong the next. None of these moments seemed to last very long.

'We're moving you,' Miss Colfield, the fat nurse, said one morning. 'A friend is going to drive you down. I'll ride along.'

I did not know or understand what she meant until the next morning when I was carried out to the car. Joan was sitting behind the wheel. My heart kicked over.

'Good morning,' she said.

'Good morning,' I said. I felt suddenly happy.

It was a beautiful ride south. We drove through Kent and down through the New Forest and I looked out at the fields and trees and hills and sunlight and knew suddenly how glad I was to be alive and how happy I was sitting here with Joan.

'How did you arrange it?' I asked.

'She did,' Joan said and smiled at Miss Colfield.

I wanted to touch Joan but could not move my hands.

'Miss Colfield,' I said, 'could we stop along the way for a drink? Even ginger beer?'

She nodded so we stopped at the next country pub and when Miss Colfield went inside I turned to Joan.

'How do you feel?' she asked.

'Fine.'

'How're your hands?'

'I wish I could use them right now.'

She kissed my face but I could not move to embrace her. Her lips were cool and soft. I did not say anything. She sat very still. Too still. I did not want to start everything again but I did not want to lose her.

'Jack,' she said. 'What do I say?'

'I'm crazy about you. You know that.'

'I thought you were playing a game.'

'I was.'

'There's no need for it with me.'

I leaned over. It hurt my legs. I kissed her.

'You had the wrong idea about me,' I said.

She laughed. 'I doubt that,' she said.

'Miss Colfield must be making the ginger beer personally.'

'Fine,' Joan said. 'What happened? I mean . . .'

37

'I don't know,' I said. 'It all happened too fast.'

She turned her head. 'Why did you come back to see me?'

'I guess I was a little crazy about you from the beginning.'

'You're conceited, aren't you?'

'No, just sure of myself,' I said, but I did not feel any of this now. It was all gone. The sea and the fire and the pain had taken all the confidence out of me. I thought suddenly of having to fly again and sitting there I was scared.

'You don't have much respect for women, do you?'

'I'm careful.'

'That's hardly an answer.'

'I think it is.'

'Darling,' she said. 'I love you.'

'And I love you, Joan.'

Miss Colfield came back with the ginger beer. We drove on to the new hospital, and the pain came back as we neared the hospital. I felt worn out and I did not care about anything in the world when we drove up the hospital drive. The pain was suddenly almost more than I could bear.

The first week there was long and dreary. I felt caged. I could not move my hands. I lay on my back all day and listened to the noises in the hospital, the gongs for the meals. Each gong marked the passing of days, of time, of hours and hours that seemed to drag on and on.

And the pain was still there when I did not have morphine. When the pain was bad I sweated, thinking if it would stop I would be happy the rest of my life. Somewhere near the hospital was a Spitfire squadron and I could hear the snarl of their engines as they passed over and I began to long to fly again, thinking of the freedom of being out of here, wondering if I would ever hold my hands on a control wheel again.

One afternoon the nurse told me a famous plastic surgeon from America was coming in to see me in the morning. That afternoon they gave me an anesthetic and removed the tannic acid from both hands.

The plastic surgeon was a tall, fattish gentleman who seemed at once personally friendly and yet very efficient and objective.

He shook his head when he looked at my hands. There were two other doctors with him. I could see my hands curling down into the palms. He clicked his tongue and shook his head.

'Septicemia,' he said and the other doctors made notes. After they left I was told that the plastic surgeon would operate on both hands in the morning.

They took me out early in the morning and gave me ether and again I dreamed that Cuddington was being shot down in flames. I saw the night fighter coming toward his bomber, low and under the tail, hanging on its propellers, sighting straight between the engines, straight into the blind spot. I had a horrible feeling that I could not warn him. Then I heard myself screaming at the tail gunner to tell Cuddington. But it was too late. The German night fighter fired a long burst into the belly and the bomber slowly blossomed into a huge flower of fire and I woke up screaming.

'Now, now,' the nurse was saying. She and another nurse were holding me down on the bed. 'You're all right.'

'He's dead,' I heard my voice saying, panting at them. 'He's dead.'

Then again the morphine killing all pain, filling my mind with strange-colored dreams.

I was so sure Cuddington was dead that when he came to see me two days later I thought I was having another nightmare. He stood in the doorway smiling. I saw he was carrying a bottle.

'God,' I said. 'I was so sure you were dead.'

'Not quite,' he grinned and set the bottle down on the floor under the bed. 'Lanson's '29. The boys sent it down.'

'Where've you been?'

'They wouldn't let anybody come down sooner.'

'How goes it?' I asked.

'Rough. Three nights in a row this week. Frankfurt, Hamburg, Stettin.'

'Have you got the G-box yet?'

'No. A couple of four-engine squadrons have.'

'Four engines?'

'Right. We'll be on them when you get out.'

'With these meat hooks I'll never fly again.'

'You need some champagne.'

He reached under the bed, unscrewed the cork. I heard it pop. He held the bottle up and I tilted my head back and he poured it down my throat. It was very dry wine. I felt lightheaded at once.

He drank and I looked at his face. His eyes looked strained.

'Had any leave?' I asked.

He shook his head. 'Too many green crews. We're flying circuits and bumps with them, breaking them in.'

'What's new in London?'

'Helene is difficult.'

'Do you see Joan?'

'They're both very busy.'

'What the hell do they do?'

'Beats me,' Cuddington said.

The floor nurse came in.

'Sir,' she said. 'Drinking is not allowed here.'

The bottle was poised at Cuddington's lips.

'Sir, I'll call the doctor.'

The nurse went out. Cuddington opened the window behind my bed and dropped the bottle out. A few minutes later one of the doctors came in.

'All right, lads,' he said. 'The nurse says you're drinking.' He tried to sound severe and formal.

'Why, sir,' Cuddington said with exaggerated innocence, 'she must mean another room.'

'Listen, lads,' he said. 'I have enough trouble with these nurses.'

He looked at Paul and then said in a loud voice that could be heard down the corridor: 'This type of conduct will not be tolerated.' Then he went out.

Paul looked at his watch. 'I've got to hit the road.'

'On tonight?'

He shook his head. 'Stand down. We lost five kites this week.'

'Five?' I said, and again the new fright that I had not known before came back to me and again the thought of flying scared me and I did not want to think about it.

He picked up his hat. 'See you next week,' he said.

'Say hello to the gang.'

He did not look at me.

'Right,' he said and went out. After he was gone I

thought that maybe there wasn't much left of the gang at the mess, that perhaps Paul was the only one of the old crowd.

They operated again a week later, ether and morphine killing my body again, and then slowly I seemed to come back to life, for they began to cut down on my morphine injections. I even began to think differently. The fear seemed gone, though I knew it was still there, but it was easier now to put it out of mind.

The day Joan came down to see me I was allowed outside and we sat out on the lawn, under the trees, looking across the Downs toward the sea. I was very happy when she was with me. She touched my hair and neck when I kissed her.

'I'm crazy about you.'

'I love you too,' I said.

The sky was red with sunset and the fields below were darkening under the trees.

'Jack?'

'Yes, darling.'

'Are you worried about flying again?'

'Not at all.'

'Then what's the matter?' she asked. 'You're so quiet.'

'Why don't you tell me what you do?'

'I can't,' she said.

'What's worrying you?'

'Nothing,' she said.

'Something is.'

She looked away. 'I was wondering, that's all. How long this will last . . . being together, I mean.'

'I don't know,' I said. 'I don't know.'

From high overhead came the faint thunder of the first bomber going out on an evening raid. The shadows lengthened; light failed through the trees.

CHAPTER SEVEN

'You're ready for another operation,' the surgeon said. He stood beside my bed. I did not mind going into surgery again. It meant that I would have convalescent leave in London if the operation was successful.

The nurse drew down the covers on my bed. The tannic acid was gone now and the skin on my legs and hands was milk white.

He looked carefully and nodded his head. Then it was morning, the next day, and the orderly came in with the needle and put it in my arm and the world became green and I slept and woke and felt my arms and hands tingling. And then the long days began, waiting for each day to pass, depressed and bored, wanting to be out of the hospital. I had not heard from Joan in two weeks and I was worried about her. I thought of her every night before I slept.

I had a flat, let-down feeling when the head surgeon told me I could have two weeks convalescent leave in London or wherever I wanted to go. I was suddenly tired with the thought, though I had looked forward to going. I wanted to see Joan, but why, if I wanted to see her, did I have this deep feeling of futility? I was tired. That must be it. I went up to London and phoned her and neither she nor Helene were home and the war office would only say that they were away and were expected back shortly. I got drunk two nights in a row with some fellow Americans who were celebrating the United States' recent entry into the war. On the third night I called Joan again. She was home. We had a wonderful time on that leave. She said she had been away in the north of Scotland on detached duty. We went out to lunch and dinner together every day.

I would pick her up in a taxi at the war office just before noon and we would kiss excitely in the back of the taxi. I had a room at a hotel on Half-Moon Street. We had our favorite places for lunch and dinner. There was a small private club just off Berkeley Square. I was a member and we used to go there first for a martini and then walk across

Berkeley Square and up Curzon Street into Shepherd's Bar where we ate lunch. In the evening after work I would meet her in the back bar of the Café Royal and we would have a drink there and then ride the bus down to Cheyne Walk along the Thames.

'When are we going to be married?' I asked her one night. She looked at me and smiled as if I had made a joke and then she saw I was serious.

'I can't,' she said. 'Not yet.'

'What's the matter?'

'I just can't.'

'I don't get it,' I said, annoyed.

'Please don't ask me.'

'I want to know.' I tried to speak lightly but it did not sound that way. 'Have you somebody in France?'

She shook her head and kissed me. 'Please,' she said. 'Please. I love you but we can't now. Not now.'

'At least tell me why not.'

'You do love me?'

'Very much,' I said.

'Then trust me. Please.'

'All right. All right,' I said because I did not want to think about anything going wrong between us.

'I'm thirsty, darling.'

'Let's go over to the White Horse.'

It was a good leave. I couldn't have asked for better. In the mornings I read the papers sitting in Berkeley Square and then walked down to Leicester Square to an American movie. There were several American war films. They all seemed fantastic and unreal, like fairy tales. Then I would go over to the Eagle Club in Charing Cross Road. There you could find out what was happening to American friends in the RAF, who was alive and who was dead. The women who ran the club knew most of the American fliers and could tell you all the latest news of your friends.

The war was moving slowly that summer even though the Americans were in it. On the Fourth of July the Americans conducted their first bombing raid, using Boston bombers for a low-level attack. I read about it in *The Times*, sitting in the Eagle Club. It made good publicity but it would be at least a year before they could stage a heavy bomber raid of any size. Perhaps in a year

43

and a half there would be both day and night raids. It would be tricky operating day raids deep into Germany. An awful amount of men would die in any such operation. Then how long would it be before we could invade the continent? The end of the war was a long way off.

I went outside and walked over to the Café Anglais and sat down at one of the tables outdoors and ordered a drink. Some American fliers that I knew came along and we spent the afternoon catching up on old times.

That night when I picked Joan up she seemed quiet and depressed.

'I'm glad you didn't bring your friends along,' she said. 'I'm not in the mood for company.'

We were in a taxi going up the Strand and she had her head on my shoulder, her eyes closed.

'Now that you mention it,' I said, 'you don't seem to be in the mood for anything tonight. What's bothering you, Joan?'

'I have to go away,' she said.

'Where?'

'It's the work I'm doing.'

'Where are you going?'

'Wales.'

'I'll try to get down,' I said.

She shook her head. 'No. You can't.'

'I'll get leave.'

'I wouldn't be able to see you anyway.'

'Why not?'

'Please, darling, trust me.'

'Why the big secret?'

'I told you. It's the work I'm doing.'

'What kind of work?'

'Believe me. I'll be back in a week.'

'Sure,' I said.

I tried to forget it that evening but we had a rotten time. I had never believed I would be so much in love and so jealous. I did not want to believe there was anybody else. Oh, to hell with it. She was taking her work too seriously. But what was it? Why couldn't she talk about it? Who was it? Was there somebody else?

'Martini?' I said.

Cuddington nodded.

I leaned on the bar in Shepherd's and signaled the bartender and told him what we wanted. He brought the drinks. They were terrible martinis. The British couldn't make martinis. They would never know how.

'Cheers,' Cuddington said.

It was almost two months since I had seen him. It seemed like centuries. He had flown many more ops since I had seen him. Even in that short time something had changed him. He looked as if he were trying to hold something together inside himself. His smile was a little too strained. He looked very tired, more tired than I had ever seen him. I stood there awkwardly. I felt very young and inexperienced beside him and I had the feeling that I had never been on operations before in my life. He seemed years older.

He drank and I drank and he did not say anything. He had phoned me that he would be in London and wanted to see me. He had heard I was on leave before the final operation on my hands. We sat down beside the window and put our glasses on the table and looked at the crowd. Again I had the feeling we both wanted to say something, only somehow there was nothing to say. Then he spoke suddenly, straight-faced, remembering an old comedy dialogue we used to work in the mess. It was so bad we always laughed at it when we got it going.

'Man's best friend?' he said quietly and slowly.

'Dog?'

'No.' He shook his head slowly, his face expressionless.

'Horse?'

'No.' He shook his head solemnly.

I stared at him blankly.

'Male alligators,' he said slowly.

'Male alligators?' I asked with exaggerated amazement.

'Female alligators lay millions of eggs. Male alligators – man's best friend – eat the eggs. If it weren't for them we'd be up to our ass in alligator eggs.'

But this time it didn't work. We couldn't seem to kid it out right.

He finished his drink in a single swallow.

'Another?' I said.

'Double.'

I ordered two double martinis. He drank the second one

in two long slow swallows, putting his glass down once between swallows. Whatever was on his mind wouldn't come out.

'How's Joan?' he asked, but he was only making conversation. There was something else on his mind.

'Fine,' I lied. 'Do you still see Helene?'

He shook his head, picked up his empty glass, stared at it. He sat there for a long moment, then he put the glass down and leaned forward.

'MacKenzie got it the other night,' he said quite suddenly. 'I could have stopped him. I could have stopped the whole bloody thing.'

Ian MacKenzie was the squadron wing commander. He had flown Spitfires during the Battle of Britain, and when they were going to ground him for being an old fighter pilot because he was thirty-two, he transferred to bomber command. He held a regular commission in the RAF and he was the only pilot I had ever seen who seemed able to navigate at night over the continent almost without consulting his navigator. He knew all the twists and turns in the Alps, all the valleys where you run down on Milan and Turin and in full moonlight he could pinpoint his way from peak to peak and valley to valley without checking either a map or his navigator. He had flown seven years before the war. He had never flinched from leading the squadron on the roughest missions and his log book held very few targets regarded as pieces of cake. I had seen him lose an engine halfway to the target and still press home the attack. Now he was dead.

Cuddington had eaten the olive off his toothpick and now he was slivering the toothpick with his thumbnail. He looked at his hands as he spoke.

'Everybody's too quiet on the squadron. God, you wouldn't know the old gang. Same old kites and they're sending us out every other night. They're kicking hell out of us with night fighters. We've got to convert to four engines or we're finished. You knew Ian. He was always doing too much. Circuits and bumps at night to break in new pilots and then flying ops. He had the flu for two weeks and wouldn't stay down. Fainted over the controls last week when he was landing.'

Now the toothpick lay in the palm of his hand in small

broken slivers. He still picked at the small slivers with his thumbnail, as if he might even split them.

'You see,' he said, 'I told him I would fly special reconnaissance for him. I even told the M.O. he ought to ground him but he got around the M.O.' Suddenly Cuddington's voice ceased. He looked up briefly and then down again at his hands, busy with the broken toothpick, and when he spoke again his voice was filled with embarrassment.

'I didn't want to. It was a hell of a target. Essen. Christ! You know what that place is like! I didn't want to fly special reconnaissance for him but he was sick. I told him I would but I didn't insist. I should have pressed him. I should have called the group captain.'

'How do you know he didn't bail out?'

'Dodd saw him. First the searchlights got into him and then a night fighter got underneath him. He never saw it. Blew him to hell. You can't see those damn night fighters if they get underneath and they won't approach any other spot.'

He paused and dropped the slivers on the table.

'But how could I have been sure?' he added. 'How can anybody ever be sure? Maybe he would have bought it the next night walking into a bus in the blackout.'

'I let a friend fly for me one night at OTU and he crashed and killed my whole crew on take off. He wanted to get the time in,' I said.

'Let's have another drink,' he said.

'Sure,' I said, thinking of Joan, wondering where she was, feeling only a profound and deep loneliness, wanting to feel regret for Ian, but feeling only my own petty loneliness.

'Are you coming to the funeral?' Cuddington asked.

I nodded my head.

Before the column reached the road that circled the airfield, the bagpipes wailed. From above the company of Highland Light Infantry, the thin high notes of the pipes streamed back upon the still air like the wild crying of dying animals. There was no sound in the sky, only the crying of the pipes, mournful and profound. We marched behind the pipers. We passed the squadron office buildings.

Ahead the morning sunlight bathed the flying field in soft warmth. We marched slowly, the slow march of the dead. The flag-draped catafalque moved slowly behind the horses. The sky glared down, pale, vividly blue, like glass.

The wailing of the bagpipes ceased. Into the silence came only the single sound of marching feet, sullen and muffled.

Ahead the bagpipers turned onto the road that circled the field. I looked across the field at the bombers parked under the trees, feeling shame and regret, thinking, *I wish I were back here*, saying it over and over in my mind: *I should be here . . . I should be here . . .* Yet scared that soon I would have to fly again. The field stretched empty, deserted.

Only the muffled sound of marching feet. Then above this sound rose the music of the pipes, high and thin. The catafalque turned onto the paved road. For a moment it paused at the turn, flag-draped, bearing a single wreath.

Then the whole column moved. As I turned onto the road I saw three women in black, with black veils over their faces, standing with heads bowed as the column passed. Mother, wife and sister. As the pipes ceased, their keening cries rose in anguish, sharp and terrible, and then swept away into the sunny air as the pipes began to play again.

The column went on. Sunlight lay thickly over everything. The sky was a curved dome of glass. The sound of the women mourning continued, their sobbing mounting to a furious animal wail that seemed to pass completely out of the realm of human grief straight into the crescendo of bagpipes.

The column moved steadily across the field with the sun rising higher. The golden all-encompassing glare of the noon sun poured down. The wind in the field beyond the column was quieting, as though waiting for silence of another realm.

The roofs of the little town beyond the field were visible between the thin green trees.

'Ian must've picked this spot,' Cuddington said. 'We just passed two pubs.'

Then the church came into view, spire first, sticking up across the flat fields, above the red-tiled roofs of the square

48

stone houses. It was an old church, an old town; a hamlet. It might have been six or seven hundred years old.

The road curved and the head of the column turned, vanishing slowly behind the row of trees on each side of the road. The bagpipes ceased, and from beyond the trees, filling the air, completely, came the sound of Rolls-Royce Merlin engines being tested for tonight's raid. The first explosive snarl of the engines seemed to rush out upon the pale sunny stillness like the roar of artillery fire; upon that blasting, snarling engine roar the thought of tomorrow rushed into mind with a sense of despair and old disasters, like old dead echoes.

Then the sound of the engines faded, almost died, became a steady, faint vibration. The bagpipes wailed again. The column passed between rows of small, gray stone houses. In the doorways the occupants leaned, their faces grave, musing, with a curious expression that was almost akin to suspicion. The bagpipes faded, died. The column turned into the front of the churchyard, stopped in the grassy graveyard behind the church. The pallbearers, lifting the coffin from the catafalque, stumbled. The spire jutted up against the sunny sky, above the ranked figures surrounding the open grave.

Suddenly the air was soundless, windless. The group stood, watching the chaplain at the head of the grave, his face smooth and serene above the little book he now held in both his hands.

The grave yawned downward into its own cool gloom of moist earth, like a steady blank face staring up at the group of bowed figures. I felt myself sway at the edge of the grave. Feeling dizzy, I stared into the black earth in the bottom of the grave. Cuddington's hand touched me.

The chaplain's voice rose, soaring over the bowed heads. It went on in the sunlight, full and soft; then it began to die away, fading into the sunny noon air.

There was a clash of metal and wood. I watched the pallbearers slowly lower the coffin. Somewhere a bugle blew, slow, mounting notes, echoing in the distant hot stillness, inevitable with tomorrow and death.

Then the column was forming up again, bagpipes bobbing along the dusty road. I looked at the people in the open doors of the small houses. Above them, seemingly beyond the town, the bagpipe music rose, soaring into the golden light of afternoon. It gave me a sudden ease, an illusion of old strength and confidence. *I'll fly all right*, I thought. *I'm not afraid.*

CHAPTER EIGHT

In the morning I returned to the hospital and two days later I had my final operation. Under the ether I had the dream again of burning, the oxygen on fire, but the dream did not last long. After the operation my hands healed quickly. Within three weeks I was taking therapy treatments. All I wanted was to see Joan again. She did not answer my letters. Twice I phoned her but nobody knew where she was. Finally one afternoon she phoned from London. It was two days before I was to be released and return to the squadron so I told her to meet me in London.

I went up to London the next afternoon. I could stay until late Sunday night. Just so I was back at the squadron Monday morning. The trains going north would be jammed on Sunday night. I had a new kit bag. I checked the bag at the Eagle Club in Charing Cross Road and took a taxi to the Ritz. I saw Joan sitting at the bar downstairs. We had a drink together and then went outside and walked across Piccadilly to the Green Park Hotel. There was a new man behind the desk.

'A double room,' I said and picked up the pen to register.

'May I see your license?' the desk clerk said. I don't believe I heard him at first because I went on signing the register.

'Your license,' he said and then I heard Joan.

'Oh, really,' she said.

'Yes,' the clerk said. 'I'll have to see your license.'

'We don't carry it with us,' I told him.

'It's a new rule.'

'What's the trouble?'

'Ever since the Americans came,' he said.

I looked at Joan. She looked at me and smiled.

I put the pen down on the counter.

'I'm sorry,' I told the clerk. 'We'll have to find another place.'

He shrugged. 'Ever since the Americans came,' he said again.

We went out and walked up Curzon Street to Shepherd Market. Joan was a member of a supper club on the corner and we went in. The tables were crowded. There were a lot of English women in Red Cross uniforms. They worked in the Washington Club for Americans a block away on Curzon Street.

The waiter came and we ordered drinks.

'We'll find some place,' I said after the waiter left. 'Wait a minute.' I went to the phone booth and called six hotels. All were booked up. I went back to the table and we sat there sipping our drinks. Several British army officers came, each with a girl on his arm.

'We could sleep in the park,' Joan laughed.

'We may yet,' I said. 'What about the YWCA?'

'You'd hate it,' she said.

'There's always the YM. How do you feel about that?'

'Crowded, darling.'

'Let's go for a walk,' I said.

'If you only knew,' she said quickly, almost as if under her breath.

'What?' I said.

'Nothing,' she smiled. 'Come on.' She took my arm and we went out and walked over to Piccadilly.

'Where should we go?' she asked.

'I've never slept in St. James's Park. Should we try that?'

'Yes, sir.'

It was a fair walk to St. James's Park and it was dark now. We sat on the grass and I kissed her and she put her arms around my shoulders and we lay back on the grass.

'Darling, I like this much better than any old hotel,' she said.

'Right now, you mean.'

'Are you hungry?' she asked.

'Yes,' I said but did not move. I felt her hand on my neck.

'Come on,' I said. 'Let's get a taxi and some dinner.'

We walked up to the street and I hailed a taxi. We sat back together and watched the street become the Strand.

I tapped on the glass window behind the driver and he slid the window back and I told him to go to the Mirabelle.

We walked in together. The head waiter bowed us to a table.

'Do you have anything special?' I asked the waiter.

'Sorry, sir, only the five shilling cover dinner.' He made a hopeless little shrug and smiled. 'I might manage some sole,' he said.

'Fine,' I said. We ordered drinks and he went away. The room was filling up. There was an orchestra playing and a few couples were dancing. The song was an old song – *Poor Butterfly*. Still, I thought, it's a better dance tune than some of the latest. I asked Joan to dance. There was something the matter. She looked unhappy. I could not imagine why and I wished it was not that way; but there was nothing I could do about it except ask and maybe find out and in some way change things for her.

The floor was not crowded. We danced in one corner. The music was loud but not too loud.

'What's the matter?' I asked.

'I feel terrible.'

I suddenly felt a premonition of disaster. 'Tell me. What is it, Joan?'

'Nothing.'

'I know something's wrong.'

'No. Really.'

'You might as well tell me.'

'I can't. I'm not supposed to.'

'Why not? What is it?'

'You mustn't tell anyone.'

'All right.'

'I can't. I'm afraid, darling.'

'Joan, please.'

'I can't. I can't. Oh, God, I have to drop again soon. I dropped when you were in the hospital. I dropped when you thought I was in Wales.'

'Dropped?'

'Parachute,' she said. 'Intelligence.'

'My God,' I said. 'Why didn't you tell me? I thought it was some other fellow.'

I suddenly felt so relieved I almost laughed but I could

52

see her face in the light shining from the ceiling. She still looked tense and upset.

'How long?' I asked, amazed. Not this small slim woman in my arms! Parachute jumping?

'Over a year,' she said.

'How many drops have you made?'

'Three.'

'What do you do?'

'I operate the radio and I come back out as a courier. I don't stay longer than two weeks.'

'I never heard it.'

'You mustn't. I wanted you to know. I didn't want you to think there was somebody else.'

'You're my girl,' I said, holding her tight, feeling closer to her than ever before.

'When do you go again?'

'I don't know.'

'How many drops do you have to make?'

'What do you mean?'

'Isn't there any limit?'

She shook her head. 'As long as we're useful.'

I felt my voice going flat. I did not want her to hear it. It was a little like not wanting your flying partner or crew members to hear your voice if it were shaky suddenly. So I danced on without speaking.

'How do you get back?' I asked after a while.

'Submarine. Offshore pickup.'

'When do you think you'll go again?'

She lifted her head. 'When's your next op?'

I smiled. 'Does Helene do it too?' I asked.

'No. She may later.'

'What ever—' I began.

She smiled and put one finger to her lips.

'Darling, you're a terrible dancer,' she said.

We woke in the dark. It was cold. The grass was cold. We had tried every hotel in London and could not get a room so all night we sat in Green Park and finally slept on the grass. We walked up to Hyde Park Corner and at one of those all night tea wagons we ate breakfast, standing on the sidewalk drinking scalding hot tea and eating Cornish pasties. It was the tea wagon whose proprietor had once posted a sign on the side, BY APPOINTMENT TO H.R.H., after the Prince of Wales had stopped one champagne dawn for hot tea. The police took the sign down. The prince was getting to be an old man now in the West Indies.

We walked along Piccadilly in the early morning light and bought all the Sunday newspapers from the sidewalk vender outside the Green Park tube station. We stood on the corner.

'What about the Washington Club?' I said. 'We might get some real breakfast there.'

'There's a war on, don't you know?' she said in exaggerated cockney.

'Listen, buster,' I said with an exaggerated American accent, 'we bailed you out of the last war but you're not going to kill us with powdered eggs.'

'They're your eggs.'

'Lend-lease. They're all yours.'

The barrel organ grinder was coming up the street. With him was his partner, carrying a small soprano saxophone. Every Sunday morning they pounded out *Underneath the Arches* below the windows of the Washington Club and the G.I.'s tossed shillings down onto the sidewalk.

We finally walked down to Leicester Square. It was a beautiful Sunday morning. We ate breakfast in a little hole-in-the-wall shop frequented by actors. They always served amazing food. I never could understand it. Baked salmon. Sole. Almost anything you wanted, while the hotels were serving bad sausage and powdered eggs. It was a small dingy room but a good breakfast. They must have had good black-market connections.

We came out onto the walk and I turned to Joan.

'Let's go up to Berkeley Square and read the papers.'

It was the best Sunday I remembered from the war. We read all the Sunday papers from the *Times* to the *News*. Later we had lunch in Chelsea at the Chelsea Arms and walked along the river by Battersea Bridge. The sun was out. We went back to Green Park and lay on the grass in the sun. But the day went quickly. I knew I had to leave soon. I looked at my watch. It was time. We caught a taxi to the Eagle Club and I picked up my kit bag.

We rode in the taxi down to St. Pancras Station.

'When do you go again?' I asked.

'They never tell us.'

'Drop me a card so I'll know.'

'No, they check that sort of thing.'

'Call me when you get back.'

'When can you get away?'

'I won't have leave for three months,' I said.

'I'll come up week ends.'

'Do you love me?'

'Oh, darling, I wish you didn't have to go back,' she said.

She was leaning back against my arm. I looked at her eyes. She looked afraid of so many things at that moment.

'There's nothing I can do about it,' I said. 'I'm afraid the old dodge about a bomb on the track won't work any more. It's like the dead grandmother.'

'What's that?'

'In America if there's an especially good ball game you use the I've-got-to-go-to-my-grandmother's-funeral to get off from work. It's somewhat overworked.'

There was a hotel across the street from the station. I rapped on the window behind the driver's head and told him to stop there. The walls of the building were flaking and chipped and pitted from bomb explosions.

Inside at the bar it was quiet, almost deserted. We drank a couple of ales and went out and I called a taxi for her.

'I'll go to the train with you.'

'No, go back now before it's dark. You'll never get a taxi otherwise.'

I took her arm and walked with her to the taxi. I pressed her hands. They were shaky. We kissed standing against the open door of the taxi. Then she got in and leaned out through the window.

'Good-bye, darling,' she said quickly. Then turning to the driver: 'Sixteen Kensington Place.'

'Good-bye,' I said. She waved and I saw her turn her face away and the taxi started forward and went down the street.

I went into the station and stood in the bar drinking ale. Someone called my name. It was a short stocky pilot officer from the squadron. He was a Welshman.

'Hello, Dai,' I said. He stood beside me and ordered a drink. He was very short.

55

'Where've you been?' I asked.

'Out and around.'

'Still on the squadron?'

'Just posted. I've been down at O.T.U.'

'What's it like?' I asked.

'Bloody. You live through O.T.U. you live through the war, mate.' He blinked and smiled. 'They kill more crews than the Germans.'

We had another ale before the train came. It was packed but we found a compartment. There were three sailors in it. They were home on leave and they had been saving their daily rum ration for three months. It was quite a trip home that night.

CHAPTER NINE

The new airfield was up north in Yorkshire, about ten miles from Leeds. A troop carrier drove us from the station. The country was flat, not real Yorkshire moors. It reminded me of parts of the Middle West. There was a cathedral town of Selby across the open country and the spire of the church stuck up against the sky. We went on along the highway. We passed farmers in horse-drawn carts and two cottages with a pub set between them. I checked in at the guardhouse. It was a wartime airfield. There were Nissen huts for barracks and for the mess. The country looked gray and dreary. I felt a hundred years old.

I walked over to the Nissen hut to which the adjutant had assigned me. I passed an outdoor latrine. It was roofless. I wondered if they were already using the wooden roofs for firewood in the stoves. You either froze or roasted in a Nissen hut. The temperature couldn't be regulated. I opened the door and dumped my kit bag on the floor. There were two iron cots in the room and a small pot-bellied stove in the center of the floor. I sat down on one of the beds. Footsteps sounded along the hall and Cuddington came in.

'My God,' he said. 'I'd given you up.' He slapped me on the back. He looked tired. His eyes looked bloodshot and his face was thin.

'What's new?' I said.

'Everything,' he said. He sat down on the edge of the bed. He lit a cigarette. 'How do you feel?'

'Fine.'

'Really fixed you up?'

'The works,' I said.

'How're your hands?'

I clenched and unclenched my fingers. The skin felt tight across the knuckles and it did not look like my skin. It was too light and made me look as if I hadn't washed well above my wrists.

'How do you feel about flying?' he asked.

'Fine,' I lied.

'Did you see the new kites?'

I shook my head.

'Four engines,' he said. 'Lancasters.'

'How are they?'

'Bloody fast.'

'How long did it take you to convert?'

'You'll be on ops before you know it. About twenty hours at night and off you go.'

He smiled.

'Any spare crews around?' I asked.

'You can pick up a crew in a day. You haven't been up in four engines yet, have you?'

'No.'

'It's very different. You have to watch it. We lost two green crews on take-off last night. Collided in the pattern.'

'Oh,' I heard myself say. I did not look at him. I reached for the package of cigarettes on the table and lit one. I thought about Joan. I thought about London. I thought about the war. I did not feel patriotic. I did not feel I wanted to go on flying. I knew I had to but I was afraid I would do the wrong thing once I got into the air. I had changed since I had been wounded. I had been scared before but not like this.

'Did you see Joan?' he asked.

'Quite a lot.'

'Good,' he said. And now he did not look at me. He blew a cloud of smoke and looked at the wall.

'How do you feel?' I asked.

'Cheesed, if you really want to know,' he said. 'I could

57

use some leave.' He snapped ash from the end of his cigarette onto the floor.

'What's the trouble?'

'We lost four planes on one op last week.'

'What was the target?'

'Stuttgart. Christ! I flew four ops last week and checked out three new pilots.'

'What about Berlin?' I asked.

'These Lancs will make it round-trip in under seven hours.'

'Have you been yet?'

'Started last week. Ran into a cold front north of Kiel and had to abort. How's your love life?'

'Haven't any.'

'Don't con me. That Joan is—'

'Iceless whiskey's ruining you.'

He just laughed.

Two nights later I went off with Cuddington on a cross-country flight. I was scared while he was checking me out. I was ham-handed on the controls. I overshot four landings.

'Take it easy,' he said slowly.

We made another circuit. I tried to relax. It would not come. I was coming in too high. A red light flashed from the ground.

'You're too high,' Cuddington said. 'Go around again.' His voice was patient.

I pushed the throttles forward. My hands froze on the control wheel. I made two circuits and felt I could not land the plane. Cuddington landed it himself.

'What's the matter?' he asked casually. We taxied off the end of the runway.

'I don't know,' I said. 'I guess that dive shook me.'

'Didn't you ever dive before?'

'Not in the channel.'

He laughed at me.

'Come on,' he said. He whacked me on the shoulders. 'Take her around once yourself. If you have trouble in the circuit, go around again.'

'Okay,' I said. I felt scared to death, as if it were my first solo. He seemed suddenly faraway. I wanted to call to

58

him. I watched him unfasten his Sutton harness and slide out of the cockpit. He went down behind me and along the fuselage and let himself out the side door.

I taxied around the perimeter track and back into the wind. I felt sweat on the back of my hands. I don't think I had ever been this scared in combat. I was suddenly petrified with fear and I had flown hundreds of hours. I took off. I was jerky and rigid at the controls.

I made two circuits and suddenly thought that I could not land the plane. I felt as if I were breaking up right in the air and then I thought suddenly of being grounded, of being cut off from friends, from Cuddington, from coming back alive and exhilarated from an ops. I thought of sitting in a chair, of living the rest of my life regretting this moment, this instant.

I began to curse and swear at myself. I turned into the funnel of lights marking the mouth of the runway ahead. I was too high. A red light flashed from the ground. I felt the plane stalling and slammed on throttles and went around again.

I flew low and turned in and began to throttle back. Sweat clung cold to my flesh. I watched the runway lights rush upward faster and faster. *Get the wheel back. Get it back!* Suddenly I had the wheel back and she was touching down smoothly.

I took off again. I felt wonderful, elated, like a new person. I had flown again. I wouldn't have to go back ashamed of myself, sitting at a desk, telling myself I could have done it if only I had tried once more. I had done it. I turned at five hundred feet after taking off. My hands held the control wheel leisurely. I landed smoothly again. Cuddington was in the mess. As I opened the door he was standing at the bar. He looked over his shoulder and smiled. He pointed at a pint of beer on the bar. I walked over to it and drank.

He grinned. 'Those kites cost the taxpayers a lot of money.'

'That's what worried me,' I said.

'Okay?'

'Okay,' I said.

CHAPTER TEN

It was a month later.

'How do you feel about it,' I asked Cuddington.

'Have you ever been near the place?' he said.

'Not low.'

'Well, cheers.' He lifted his glass. 'I'm going to get a new rabbit's foot. That old black silk stocking you stole from a virgin at midnight is just about run out of luck. We're going to need something new.'

'Ah, it'll be a piece of cake,' Craddock said.

'Sure,' I said.

'In a Lanc as low as you'll be, they'll never swing fast enough to hit you with heavy flak,' Craddock said.

'I don't mind the heavy stuff,' Cuddington said. 'But have you seen the recon photos of the light flak installations? Bofor barrels. It looks like an orchard.'

'We'll be in and out before they know what's happening,' I said.

Cuddington laughed. 'Wait'll we start climbing over those flak alleys beyond the target.'

'I still think our speed will take care of everything at low level.'

'We'll find out,' Cuddington said.

'Don't forget how we got out of Cherbourg through all those damn ship masts.'

'Cherbourg,' Cuddington said. 'That piece of cake!'

We were in London on this particular Saturday night. We were in Shepherd's Bar, just off Curzon Street. There were some American fliers sitting at the next table to us. The place was full of smoke and noise and drinking.

'Where do you get that crap?' an American captain said. 'What do you mean, Cherbourg's a piece of cake? You Limey bastards, flying around in the dark so the Germans can't see you to shoot at you! Where do you get that crap?'

'That's right,' Cuddington said. 'A piece of cake.'

'A piece of cake?' The American captain was shouting now. 'Since when did you Limeys ever raid Cherbourg in daylight? Flying around at night for three years. I'd like to get you up in a Fortress during the day. If you ever saw a Focke-Wulf before sundown you'd die of fright.'

'Righto,' Cuddington said. 'And you've been here almost six months now and haven't flown across the Rhine yet. When's your bloody air force going to raid a German target? Are you going to win the war bombing Frenchmen?'

We got up and left. Cuddington didn't give a damn any more what he said to anybody.

We were rehearsing now at Westheath Airfield up in Norfolk for a special mission.

It was beautiful country. The weather was sunny and we could hunt grouse almost every evening. But Cuddington was jumpy and cross. We were flying together now. He had begun to get nervous about engine maintenance. Craddock was a warrant officer, and he was in charge of maintenance on our aircraft. After we'd been in London, Cuddington began to double check Craddock on every little screw and bolt in the plane and question him about it each day.

One evening we landed after a practice flight. We'd been out over the North Sea practicing low level, running up to the coast and then in low over the land and out again. Cuddington was never reckless or wild, but he could get down on the deck lower than anybody. Coming back one of the engines missed a little. We landed and went into the mess. Craddock was standing at the bar.

'Craddock,' Cuddington said. 'You better see the old man tomorrow about working on another aircraft.'

'What?'

'I don't want you working on our engines any more.'

'You'll wish you were kidding when you get over that target.'

'Okay,' Cuddington said. 'But I'm not kidding now.'

The next day Craddock put in for a transfer.

That night I was in the mess lounge with Cuddington when Wing Commander Baker came in.

'Beer?' Baker asked.

'No,' said Cuddington. 'No thanks.'

'Good weather tomorrow,' I said. 'We'll get in plenty of time.'

'I suppose so,' Cuddington said. I didn't know what he was thinking about, but it wasn't like him not to be interested in flying.

Baker finished reading the paper and got up and went out. I sat there.

'How'd the engines sound today?' Cuddington asked me.

'Okay.'

'And how was my flying?'

'What the hell are you asking me for?'

'I want to know.'

'You're off,' I said. 'A little off.'

'I never felt like this before.'

'Forget it,' I said.

'I never used to.'

'What's the trouble?' I asked.

'I don't know.'

'Come off it.'

'Honest to God, I never felt like this before.'

'How's Helene?'

'Fine,' he said quickly.

'Maybe you ought to take a couple of days off. Go and see her.'

'That isn't it.'

'You better eat something,' I said.

'I don't feel like it,' he said.

He wasn't sharp all that week. He looked as if he were flying low without thinking about it.

About the middle of the next night, the light went on in my room and Cuddington was standing there under the light bulb suspended on a cord from the ceiling. I didn't know the time.

'Morning already?' I said.

'No. I can't sleep.'

'Look,' I said. 'It's another target, that's all. They picked you because you're the best low-level pilot in the air force and you've gone in this low before and they need you again, because they figure you're the only guy who can do it right. I'm just excess baggage as second pilot. This isn't any worse than the others you've pulled alone. Forget it. Go to sleep.'

'I can't sleep,' he said. 'You know, I never thought about

surviving before. I started thinking about it lately. I shouldn't, but it's there and I can't stop it. I think about not dying. About living through this war. About getting married and having some kids and settling down. I think about those bloody Jerries. I hate the bastards. When the hell is this thing going to stop?'

'Well,' I said, 'one way or another it'll stop two days from now. Because that's when we're going over.'

'Jesus,' he said. 'I wish I could sleep.'

His face was hard and his eyes were tired the next day. We went up high and practiced diving down on the coast. But he wouldn't come down low, not low enough for real practice. We might as well have stayed on the ground. He made a rough landing. He bounced the plane twice before he got the wheels down right.

The morning of the day before the raid, he wasn't at breakfast. When I went down to his room there was a note on his bed: *I'll be back in time to go. I'm going into town.* I went over to see Baker.

'You better get hold of him,' Baker said. 'Do you know where he stays?'

'Flemmings.'

'Well, get a jog on fast and get him back here.'

I drove down to London and found Cuddington's name in the hotel register at Flemmings. I went upstairs and knocked at the door.

'Come in,' Cuddington said. I opened the door. He lay there on the bed. He was wearing his trousers and shirt with the tie off. His tunic hung over the back of a chair. He lay there looking tired.

'Hello,' he said. 'Sit down.'

'What's up?'

'Have a drink.'

He reached for the bottle and poured me a drink in the empty glass on the night table. He held the other glass.

'Cheers,' he said. He clinked the two glasses together and handed me one.

I drank and he drank. There was a bottle of White Label on the table. He didn't say anything and I didn't say anything. We just sat there and drank in silence.

Then I poured myself another drink and poured him one. He sipped it slowly. I put water in mine. I offered to

63

get him water, but he shook his head and held his hand over his glass.

'They get some wonderful ideas up at headquarters,' he said. 'I used to wonder what they did all day up there.'

I finished my drink and set my glass down.

'Fix another drink,' he said.

'That's enough now.'

'God,' he said. 'I never used to drink this much. Bad show. Bad for track. What the hell could I have been thinking?'

'I know,' I said.

'Listen,' he said. 'This hero stuff is for the birds.'

'We'll make it all right.'

'Look,' he said. 'About Helene. If we don't make it this time, she's a widow first time out. She wants to get married before this last do. Whether you think so or not, this damn well can be our last do.'

'Why think about it that way?'

'All right, all right,' he said. 'You don't understand. Hell, I don't understand any more either.'

'It's a piece of cake,' I said.

'Sure,' he said. 'A piece of cake.'

He poured himself another drink.

'Take it easy,' I said. He lay back on the bed and set his glass on his stomach and looked up at the ceiling.

'You don't know what it's like,' he said. 'I can't sleep any more.'

'It's too late now to catch up on your sleep.'

'Hell,' he said. 'She's got the papers. We could be married this afternoon in Chelsea.'

'Marry her,' I said. 'You've nothing to lose. If you love her and get back, there you are.'

'And if I don't, where does that leave her? I could give her a baby tonight and tomorrow I don't come back. That's no way, only she can't see it. That's no way, no matter how much she loves me or I love her. And what about the kid? That's no way for him.'

He didn't move. He just lay there, looking up at the ceiling. I poured some more whiskey into his glass. I poured myself another drink. The bottle was almost empty, but it hadn't taken us any place. We were still clear and tight inside our heads. Tomorrow was too near. It was right in the room. He sat up, looked at me.

'Do you know what they want me to do? Do you know what you should do? Get off this op! Go sick!'

'Sick?'

'Do you know what's going to happen? I'm supposed to crash land the aircraft after we bomb. We're a decoy. You're not even supposed to know about it.'

'You're drunk,' I said.

'How much can they expect?' he said. 'I've been flying combat for almost five years. Damn little time off. I never asked for it. But now they want me to spend the rest of the war in a prison camp. And decoy for them, carry papers that make it look as if the Allies think this heavy-water operation we're bombing in Germany is the key one, the only one we know about.'

'Heavy water?'

'You aren't supposed to know.'

'But—'

'Give me another drink,' he said. 'We're supposed to draw attention away from the major heavy-water plant in Norway so the Allies can get in and blow it up.'

'What the hell?'

'Jerries are working on making an atom bomb.'

'Atom bomb?' I said. 'What—'

'Go sick. Get off this op. We aren't coming back,' he said.

'There's no one else,' I said. 'I've got to go.'

'The hell you do! The woods are full of second pilots.'

'I'm all set.'

'You're crazy. Go on back to the field.'

'When're you coming back?' I asked.

'Sometime this afternoon.'

'Baker's worried.'

'I'll be there.'

'Don't get drunk,' I said.

'Don't worry.'

Baker was in his office, sitting at his desk reading. He looked up.

'Did you find him?' he asked.

'He's okay.'

65

'What's his trouble?'

'A race horse relaxing. He'll be in this afternoon.'

'Righto,' said Baker.

I went out to look at our plane and check it over. About five o'clock from the mess window I saw a taxi coming up the drive from the station. Cuddington got out and paid the driver. I went into the bar. He was there drinking a pint. Baker was with him.

'All set?' I said.

Cuddington nodded.

'Everything okay?' Baker asked.

'Sure,' Cuddington said. 'I feel fine.' His face looked different, and so did his eyes now. He smiled.

'Good show,' said Baker. 'We're counting on you, you know.'

Cuddington grinned. He winked at me.

'It's a piece of cake,' he said. Baker went out.

We stood at the bar drinking beer.

'I was really screwed-up this morning,' Cuddington said.

'Forget it,' I said.

'I wish you would.'

'Sure.'

'Where'd Baker go?' he asked. He put his glass down on the bar. 'I wanted to buy him a drink.'

'He's got work to do.'

'How much did I tell you?' Cuddington asked. He began to draw a wet ring on the top of the bar with his forefinger.

The bartender picked up our glasses.

'Two pints,' Cuddington told him. The bartender went away.

'You said we were going to have to ditch the plane to the Jerries and you were going to play some kind of decoy with papers.' I thought of Joan. I couldn't tell her. I couldn't tell anybody.

'That's right,' Cuddington said.

'Hell of a place to sit out the war,' I said.

He didn't say anything.

'Drink up,' I said.

'Something's going to happen,' Cuddington said. 'I never felt this way before. I never believed in presentiment before. The Jerries don't want this target bombed. They'll throw up everything on the bomb run. It's as important to them as the Norway location.'

'This is what we signed on for,' I said. 'Don't forget it.'

'You sound like a politician,' Cuddington said. 'Don't give me a speech.'

'Just keep flying that plane and we'll be all right.'

'No,' he said. 'We've had it. They'll be waiting for us. Really waiting for us this time.'

'Maybe I ought to turn you in, or maybe you need some sleep.'

'Forget it,' he said. 'I can fly that plane better than anybody we've got.'

'Stop talking about it then!'

After supper Cuddington went to his room. I knocked on his door about eight o'clock. There was no sound. I opened the door. The light was on and he was lying on the bed. He didn't look at me.

'See you at breakfast,' he said. He was lying on his back looking up at the ceiling. I shut the door.

At breakfast, with the air still dark outside and the lights shining in the empty mess, Cuddington was silent.

After breakfast, we went over to the briefing room. It was still dark outside. The map was on the wall with the red ribbon on it connecting England with Germany. The intelligence officer finished giving us the run-down and Cuddington stood up.

'Are you sure you have the right number of guns spotted on the flak alleys leading into the target?'

'It's the latest,' the intelligence officer said.

'How long ago?' Cuddington asked.

'A week,' the intelligence officer said.

'That's the best we could do without arousing suspicion,' Baker said.

'Well, they know we're coming now.'

'The weather's good in and out,' Baker said.

'Let's go,' I said.

We went down to the flight line and got dressed. 'That weather report smells,' Cuddington said.

'You never can tell,' I said.

'Just so it holds clear going in,' Cuddington said.

'Are you going to climb to go over those hills?' Baker

asked when we were dressed and standing outside waiting for a truck.

'No,' Cuddington said. 'Low all the way.'

The truck came and we got in back and rode out along the flight line. It was chilly and dark. The sky was moonless.

Baker drove out in his car when we were putting our gear in the plane.

'You ought to make it in less than three hours,' he said.

'The engines sounded fine yesterday,' Cuddington said.

'This mission means a lot,' Baker said.

'Put some beer on ice for us,' Cuddington said. He winked at Baker.

We got in and Baker poked his head up through the hatch under the cockpit. Cuddington was doing a cockpit check and I had a map spread out on my knees. Cuddington looked down at Baker.

'So long,' I said.

'Have a good trip,' Baker said and gave a thumbs-up. Then he pulled his head out and we heard the hatch slam shut.

We taxied out and got the green light from the tower. It didn't take long to reach the coast. In the dark, the foam was a white collar against the cliffs. Then we were over the sea. The stars were out, shining in the water, and the sky above was pitch black. Without the moon, it felt as if we were inside an immense black ball, with stars surrounding us top and bottom.

The minutes ticked past. I checked our course. We were now fairly close to the French coast. In the starlight, the shadow of our plane fled over the black water. We set course north, crossed the coast. A searchlight flashed ahead, sabering the darkness, but it was too high and we were too fast.

We flew on. 'I checked our course and time,' called the navigator.

'Twenty minutes to the target,' he said.

Suddenly we were in rain, pouring rain; the rounded window of the cockpit flowed with a thousand rivulets. In the half-light of dawn, Cuddington seemed to sense the trees around us. Scraps of clouds skidded past. Suddenly the rain ceased.

The air was greenish and then once again we plunged

into a thick vapor. The ground blurred. We swung back and forth between hills. The compass turned slowly. The horizon marked rows of hills; unknown roads slipped past underneath. Any second we would emerge into a flak zone. The old terror of being low in enemy territory came over me again.

Suddenly a stream of tracer bullets shot past, close.

The warning had been sent ahead.

'Get ready,' Cuddington said.

I went down in the nose to the bombardier. Light, dawn light, was upon us, the country low and flat, with here and there a light shining out of an open door.

Then I saw the flak towers: one, two, three, four – seven flak towers!

'Look out! Flak at five o'clock!' I yelled.

Six big black puffs from eighty-eight millimeter shells appeared behind us. I looked at my watch. Fifteen seconds into the target. Fear caught my throat. My stomach contracted.

'Quick, left,' the bombardier called. That would bring us in line with the serrated roof of the building ahead. We were flying flat out, full throttle.

'Smell those flowers,' Cuddington yelled. Flak! Christ, it was all around us now. The entire ground seemed to light up with flashes from twenty-two millimeter and thirty-seven millimeter guns. There must be over a hundred. A carpet of white puffs appeared in front of us. God, what flak! My heart caught in my throat.

We went down lower into the flak smoke. Explosions and tracer bullets crisscrossed all around us. Terrible flashes.

Now we were half a mile from the building, about one hundred feet from the ground. The building rushed toward us. We were doing close to 400 m.p.h. There a tree, a street . . . then the building roof.

The roof loomed. We zoomed abruptly. To our right a wooden frame building flew into the air. A flak tower disintegrated. Suddenly a whirlwind of flames and fragments filled the sky. I put my head behind armor plating. A salvo of shells burst close. The sky flashed. A rattle of shrapnel rained on the fuselage. The flak rose all around us, tracer bullets pursuing us. I climbed back into the cockpit.

Cuddington was hanging onto the control wheel. His face was covered with sweat. His eyes widened, then rushed wild. 'Bail out!' he shouted. 'Bail out!' He pulled the plane up. It climbed, staggered, began to slip.

'Come on,' I said. 'Let's get out.'

He shook his head, leaned forward, put the nose down. Five hundred feet. We passed slowly over a field. He was going to land, belly land, crash. What the hell! Mechanically, he began to approach. Suddenly fear caught me at the throat, the vision of so many burning crashes. *God, be careful! Don't stall! Don't stall!*

Here was the ground rushing up. *Now! Now!* He rammed the nose down, and stuck one wing down to take the shock. Then a terrific jolt. We bounced and the wings vanished like tissue paper. I flung my arms in front of my face. Then a violent jerk. I felt the straps of my harness snap. I was hurled forward. I tasted blood in a blur of red light, then the crackling of fire and the burst of a shell going off.

I hacked at Cuddington's harness. He slumped over the control wheel. I caught his torn sleeve. I wrenched him out of the torn cockpit, dragged him across damp grass. The plane exploded suddenly in a dazzling burst of light.

He lay on the grass. He looked beat. 'I hope those bastards back at command are satisfied.' He shut his eyes.

'Why didn't you fly back to England?' I asked. 'That's what you really planned, wasn't it?'

He didn't open his eyes. He lay there, panting.

'The kid,' he muttered.

'What kid?' I said.

'I married Helene yesterday afternoon. It's funny how you change your mind about things when you're going to have a kid.'

'You just got married,' I said.

He opened his eyes. 'She just found out she was pregnant,' he said.

'You should have told me.'

'I started thinking over the target what it would be like if she did have the kid. I want that kid. I had to do it this way.'

70

The trouble was the plane and all the decoy papers were blown to hell. We crawled away through the grass. Machine-gun bullets from the turrets were snapping like firecrackers in the burning wreckage.

CHAPTER ELEVEN

I had not seen the German countryside before and it was strange and a little unreal to see the land we had been bombing. The earth rolled barrenly with patches of trees and hills to the west.

'Anybody get out?' I asked.

Cuddington sat holding his head between his hands. There was a bad bruise above his eye.

'I don't know,' he said. 'We better get out of here.'

He rose. We started climbing up the smooth rocky side of a ridge. It was covered with boulders. Cuddington climbed slowly with an air of dazed astonishment. From beyond the ridge that screened the burning plane, the sound of the fire rushed steadily upward and a huge gust of smoke, like an immense black balloon, rushed skyward. Cuddington stumbled among the boulders. I caught his arm.

'Come on! Come on!' he said dazedly. He thrust my arm away. 'They'll have troops in here in no time.'

'Where's your escape kit?' I asked.

Yes, he had his escape kit. He said we better find a place to hide first and then check the map. He said he thought we were some place east of the Ruhr Valley.

Halfway up the ridge, trees rose, covering the mouth of a small cave in the rock. Cuddington knelt down and crawled inside. I crawled in beside him and opened my escape kit.

He squatted, dazed.

'We better go north into Holland,' I said. I looked at the map on the floor of the cave. It was brightly colored, made of silk, like a large handkerchief; I believe after the war they were sold as such in the war surplus stores. They were very easily folded. Cuddington shook his head.

'I wouldn't mind seeing Paris,' he said, trying to smile.

'We will,' I said, 'if we make Holland.'

'Let's sack in here until it gets dark. Christ, I wonder if any of the crew got out. It was a thousand feet.'

We lay in the mouth of the cave and watched the smoke from the burning plane rising against the sky.

Cuddington said, 'My head feels like ten mornings after. Much of a cut?'

'Not too bad,' I lied. We needed the first-aid kit but there was no hope of getting it now. I studied the map again.

'We're not more than fifty miles inside Germany,' I said. I pointed at the map. 'Only five miles from town. They'll have troops out here looking for us in fifteen minutes.'

'Why not head straight north as soon as it's dark?'

'What if they've got dogs?' I said.

He shrugged. We lay in the mouth of the cave. It was past noon before we heard anything. Then came the sound of a whistle. We looked through the trees that screened the mouth of the cave. I saw men below in the valley. They all wore German helmets and they were walking in a skirmish line. There were no dogs.

'Do you see them?' I asked.

'Yes.'

We lay flat on the stone floor and looked down the slope of the ridge at the valley.

'Do you want to shoot it out and make a break for it?' Cuddington asked.

'Don't be a fool!'

'If there's only a couple and they try to take us, why not? There's woods behind us.'

'Too many of them altogether.'

'Okay.'

'It'll be dark in a couple of hours,' I said.

The skirmish line of men in German helmets skirted the ridge below us, looking up the steep rocky slope. Somewhere a whistle blew. In hobnail boots they would find it difficult climbing the smooth rocky surface below the cave. We drew our heads back into the cave.

We waited half an hour. There was no sound. We looked out. The valley below was empty.

'Let's get out of here,' Cuddington said.

'Wait'll it's dark.'

'They'll come back through us. Right over us from the other side on their way back. It's an old dodge. Overrun the target and then run in on it from another angle.'

'We'll have a better chance in the dark.'

'Okay. But I'm going to shoot if we run into them.'

'You're crazy,' I said angrily. 'What do you expect to gain? You'll only give us away.'

'Do what you want to do,' Cuddington said. I did not say anything. Maybe the bump on the head made him a little crazy. I was ready to work with him but not to throw my life away in a senseless stand against ridiculous odds.

We lay in the cave. Across the hills the sun was dying. Beyond the hills was the Dutch border. From here we could see only hills and trees. The air became cool, then chilly. The sun went down slowly, but the last light, rosy and gold, shone faintly through the dark trees on the hills beyond us.

'Look!' Cuddington said and pointed down into the valley. It was almost dark now. Below in the valley we could see flashlights moving. They moved almost as if they were suspended in mid-air. I could not see the men handling the lights. I counted them. There were about twenty. They came across the valley in a line. Somewhere a dog howled, mournful and remote in the stillness. The men below made no noise.

'Jesus!' Cuddington said. The flashlights danced in the darkness now. The dog howled. I heard Cuddington snap the safety catch off his .38.

'Give 'em a little rapid fire,' he said. 'Then break for it. They'll douse the lights. Keep moving and they'll have a hell of a time finding us once we separate.'

Against the dog he was right. With two tracks to follow, one of us might get away. The thing to do was to shoot only enough to cause quick confusion and then get out fast.

'Listen,' I said. 'When you hear them running in the woods, run with their sound and stop and then listen to them running. They'll stop. Don't move until they move. I'll do the same. It'll divide them when they hear two of us running at different times. I'll run when I hear them stop.'

'Okay,' he said. 'When I fire, fire right after me. Break to the left. I'll break right.'

73

'I'm with you,' I said. I pulled out my Webley.

I had always considered it ridiculous to carry the revolver on raids. What could you do against troops if captured? But it was not a bad habit to carry it because you never knew now what the civilians might try if they picked you up in a town you'd bombed.

As I was thinking this, Cuddington fired three shots. I saw the flashlights waver far below like miniature searchlights. Then I saw the flashes of rifles and heard the reports. I fired three times rapidly into the darkness and jumped out of the cave and scrambled up the hill into the woods.

The ground rose. The brush was thick. The moon shone through a broken cloud. The high trees looked like birch and pine.

I ran on, stopped in the dark and listened. I heard the Germans moving up the crest of the hill, entering the woods. I ran again and stopped and listened. The Germans stopped. There was no sound. I did not move. Then I heard shouts and running in the opposite direction. They were sending somebody after Cuddington. I ran again, full speed through the brush. I stopped, sat down and listened. I estimated I had run a quarter of a mile. I sat in the bottom of a ravine. It was full of brush and birch trees. I lay under one tree and listened.

There was no sound now. Even if they were not talking I would have heard them. They could not come through the brush without making noise. They must have gone after Cuddington. Fog began to rise in the ravine. It was cold and damp.

Then the dog bayed. I lay still and listened. The dog bayed again, high and clear. It ceased abruptly.

I stood up, slanted my head into the wind, listened. There was only an immense dark stillness.

I'll have to get him, I thought. I felt for the knife in the scabbard stuck in the top of my boot.

The voice of the dog came again. If the dog was ahead of the Germans I'd have to handle him with a knife. But he was probably working on a leash. There would be at least one German with him. I would have to chance it on the dog alone. I gripped the knife. The howl of the dog came closer.

74

I moved a few feet to crouch behind a larger tree. The dog howled nearby and stopped.

Something struck me in the back with a heavy blow. I fell face down. I had the knife out. I sprang up. The dog crouched, snarling, and leaped. I slashed, missing. I whirled and the dog sprang again.

I felt the knife go in. The dog screamed, flopped over on his side. The knife stuck out of his stomach. I crawled toward him on hands and knees. He snarled and whimpered. He got up, lurched, crawled away.

I heard the shot before the light struck me. I was down on one knee and the rifle crashed again in the beam of light. Then I was up and running. The gun fired again, and then, during a long moment while I ran, I heard the sharp echo of the shots coming back through the woods from far away.

I ran on, blundering through the woods. Brush raked and tore at my face. My chest began to burn inside. I ran on, panting, waiting for the crash of the rifle again. In the moonlight I saw the tree, a rotted pine shell, topless, about ten feet high, with a small opening in the bottom.

I looked back through the woods. There was a big pine tree. It was just what I wanted if I guessed right. I took off my flying boots and stuck them in the opening at the foot of the hollow stump. The toes of both shoes stuck out just far enough to be seen. The woods here were clear of brush and the moonlight shone white and clear upon the ground.

I lay down behind the big pine and covered myself with leaves. I could see the hollow high stump about fifty yards away. I listened. I began to shake with the cold of the ground. For a long while there was no sound. Then it came. At first I thought it was the wind drawing through the branches and leaves. Then it came again, a single noise, a dry, whispering sound. I began to pant, trying to hold my breath.

Then the German was there. He had come almost soundlessly. I did not know he was there until the gun crashed twice and I looked up and saw the flashlight beam.

He stood in profile about twenty yards away, the rifle against his shoulder, his head down, bucking a little with each shot. He worked the bolt fast. The flashlight was fixed to the top of the barrel like a telescopic sight.

I counted the shots until I knew he was near the end of the clip. Had I counted wrong? I lay there in quiet horror for a long second. I saw him walk toward the hollow stump. His back rose in silhouette. Now, I thought, now.

I don't remember springing, or even moving. I was running full speed before he turned. He lowered the rifle, and then he saw me. He was only a few feet away. His face ballooned suddenly.

I was off my feet as the rifle rose toward me, the barrel elongated. I clawed at the rifle like a drowning man. I heard the explosion. I'm dead, I thought, I'm dead, and then my shoulders jerked with pain and I knew I held the rifle barrel in both hands.

His eyes glared like a madman. He swung the rifle, bellowing.

I let go of the barrel and drove in with both legs spread and got both arms around his belly. We fell. I was on top of him. His breath stank of onions. I got both hands on his throat. He struck at my head with one fist. I squeezed and squeezed, pressing down upon his throat. He gurgled. His body surged.

I pressed down. His body froze under my hands. Then it surged almost erect. For an instant he was almost bolt-upright. His eyes bulged slowly. His tongue edged out between his lips. Then I felt him crumple, his whole body, from the neck down. I don't remember taking my hands from his throat. He fell backwards.

I knelt there, panting, and searched his pockets. I removed bank notes from his wallet and cartridges from a leather pouch on his belt. I picked up the rifle, loaded it, sat down, trying to catch my breath.

I lay there a long time, resting. Then I put my boots back on. In the silence I thought I heard voices in the distance. I began to breathe quietly. Then I heard the voices again. I listened. It was only a single voice, far-faint.

As I walked away the voice became clearer. I walked toward the sound of the voice. 'Help!' the voice cried in English. 'Help!'

After all that had happened it was somehow funny seeing Cuddington in the hole. It was an old rock pit, round and smooth sided. It was impossible to climb out. It was at least fifteen feet deep.

'Come on up,' I said.

'My ass is broken,' Cuddington said.

I lay on the ground and looked down into the hole. I could not see his face.

'Why don't you look where you're going?' I said. 'Are you okay?'

'Get me out!'

I cut a limb from a tree and stuck it down into the hole and drew him up.

CHAPTER TWELVE

That was a long night. We had expected to be killed at first. I was surprised we had escaped. I was still surprised when we did not hear more that night. We checked the north star and began to walk west. It was a clear moonlit night. We passed a German flak battery on the far side of a field. You could see the barrels of the eighty-eights dark and long against the light sky. We passed a town to the south, then toward dawn came on a paved road. The whole country was silent. Cuddington's head hurt him and he did not sound like himself but he kept walking. My arm was tired from carrying the rifle but we might have to use it and I still had the ammunition so I did not throw it away.

In the dark the country stretched away to the lighter horizon of the sky. The land was flat and black and there were no hills or trees. We did not talk. We walked beside the road in the grass, thinking only of moving in the darkness without making noise. We had been walking like that for an hour when, without warning, three Germans sprang out of a ditch beside the road. I saw them for an instant as they flashed a light in our faces.

I saw their pistols pointed at us. I dropped the rifle.

'Get your hands up!' they shouted in German.

There wasn't time to be surprised. One of the Germans started toward us. The other two kept the light in our faces. I stood there with my hands up. The German began to search us. Cuddington said something to him in German.

The German did not answer. He removed our revolvers. He stepped back with the other two Germans. Cuddington spoke to them again in German and one of the Germans barked an order. Again Cuddington spoke to him. His voice sounded complaining. I heard one of the Germans laugh.

'They won't fall for it,' Cuddington said.

'Where did you learn German?' I said.

'Shut up,' Cuddington said. 'I told him I couldn't see very well. If we could get one to walk ahead of—'

One of the Germans bellowed and started to move toward us. He prodded us with his pistol.

'They won't sucker,' Cuddington said.

I could see why. It was an obvious ruse. Get one to lead the way with the flashlight, push him over and, in the confusion, run from those in the rear. But they weren't buying.

Cuddington spoke to them again and one of the Germans hit him in the face. I saw his head jerk back and blood spurt on his jaw. I heard one of the other Germans shout. It was an order to stand in line ahead of them.

They grabbed us and put us in line. Cuddington walked ahead of me. They took us along a path in the field beside the road. They walked behind us and laughed and flashed their flashlight on a path ahead of us. I slowed down. If the German behind me walked too fast and bumped me I could snatch his pistol. It was our only chance. But they were experienced soldiers. The German behind me poked me in the back with his gun and laughed and said something to the others. They laughed.

'They know all the tricks,' Cuddington said.

Walking in single file we descended a hill, following a path. I looked ahead. The ruin of a bombed house rose against the starlit sky. It was lightless, desolate. A moment later, against the flat dark country, the ruined house lifted its jagged square walls.

At the dark door Cuddington protested in German and muttered to me in English. I could not understand what he said. And then I saw the steps leading down into the house. One German turned and said something to the other two. Cuddington spoke in German as if he were arguing. He stepped back so that he was behind me. He spoke to the German in a grumbling voice. The German made a guttural, snarling sound. I saw Cuddington shrug.

I stepped through the doorway. I started down the stairs. Cuddington stumbled and cursed. I heard him step again and slam the door hard behind me, and then we were in the dark. I heard the flashlight clatter down the steps outside, and break. We leaped across the dark room. The German raked the room with bullets. We broke like quail for the shattered window at the end of the room. The firing ceased. I vaulted across the window casement. A gun rattled. Another raked the field. It went on firing long after I was out of range.

At last the firing and shouting faded, died away. It was pitch dark now. The moon was covered by clouds. I did not go into the woods. Instead I ran along the edge of brush marking the boundary of the woods. An hour later, when the alarm began again, I lay out in the open in the dark beyond the woods and listened to the Germans pass and enter the woods. I did not stay long, just long enough to rub my hands to get them warm. They were half-frozen.

I began to walk slowly so as not to tire. Then it was shortly before dawn, then daylight. The air was gray and in the half-light there was a feeling of time suspended. Birds began calling, waking all around. The air tasted suddenly fresher, clean as spring water. I took deep breaths as I walked and in each breath fatigue seemed to wash away. I was amazed. I walked on faster, breathing quickly.

When daylight came I tried to keep count of the hours, estimating my walking speed with the swing of the sun. The country was open and I walked in the fields away from the roads. That night I slept in a haystack. It was dark when I woke and I lay in the hay watching a lamp being lighted in the farmhouse. Then I heard cattle bellow in the meadow below and the sound of a man walking past the haystack and then presently the sound of cattle coming back and their deeper sounds as he drove them into the nearby barn.

It was still dark when I crept up to the house and smelled smoke and food. It was a hot, delicious smell. It was in that instant that, for the first time in more than twenty-four hours, I realized I was hungry. I haven't eaten, I thought, I must eat something.

So I returned to the haystack and watched the man return to the house and waited, lying still, until the man left the house again and disappeared into the fields. Then, just as the sun's rays struck level across the field, I walked up to the house. The kitchen door was shut. I knocked and heard the woman coming to the door. I hated her in that instant because she was German and, as I thought to ask her for food, hate was suddenly even stronger than hunger. I felt the words confusing in my head with anger. Come on, come on, I told myself. You wouldn't feel this if you hadn't been shot down.

Her face was long and gaunt and the skin on her cheeks looked dried and brown. She said nothing and I said nothing for a long moment. Her eyes grew larger and shock and fear came into them. I heard my mouth saying something I could not seem to hear. She knows my uniform, I thought.

'Some bread,' I heard my mouth say. 'Have you got some bread?'

I saw her mouth move. She knew some English.

'Bread?' she said. 'Bread?' Then her face contorted suddenly with rage and she screamed at me and began shouting.

I pushed her back into the house and banged the door shut. Then I was running. I do not know how long I ran nor in what direction, and later I remember being surprised because I had run so far without tiring. In the hunger and fear of being killed I had the sensation of being quite light. I ran full speed until my foot struck something and I fell.

I had the feeling I was still running but I was lying on my stomach, looking at the ground. I looked around. I lay on the edge of a potato field and the plants stuck up greenly across the flat distance. I lay there a long time, panting. Then I knew I had to get up and go on. It was a gray day, a gray sky. I had the feeling of being turned around. I felt lost. I jerked the two middle buttons off my jacket. One button contained a small sharp point and a faint notch on its rim. The pointed fitted into the other button and together they made a compass. It was standard equipment to help fliers who were shot down. But it was dark now in the sky and I realized suddenly I had slept after falling.

But I was not disturbed. I began to walk again and I tried to remember how long I had slept and whether it had been morning or evening when I had gone to the farmhouse. It was all confused suddenly. I walked all night across fields and sometimes it seemed I had not been asleep at all. I slept again at daylight, in a ditch. When I woke it was dark and it seemed to me I had waked but I did not remember having slept and counting back, day, night, day, night, day, night, I lost track again of time, I slept again beside a stream, under a tree, and when I woke it was dark.

Then it came to me that I was hungry. I crept into the field. I felt in the dark for whatever was growing and dragged away a cabbage and sat under the tree by the stream and gnawed at the cold hard ball of cabbage. I fell asleep again and dreamed of dinners I had eaten long ago, Thanksgiving and Christmas, hot steaming mashed potatoes and giblet gravy and hot turkey and cranberry sauce and golden baked yams and dishes of celery and olives and butter and golden corn bread and mince and apple pie and whipped cream. I woke with an excruciating stomachache and drank from the stream and felt like hurling the cabbage into the water.

I was hungry all the time after that, eating rotting vegetables in the fields and potatoes hard as cold clay. I walked through two intervals of light and dark, all count of daylight and dark had been lost. I thought only of eating enormous quantities of food. I thought of the poor fare in the mess. How good it looked now in my mind, the unbuttered toast, the hot scalding tea, and unsugared flat porridge.

I traveled only at night. I kept trying to remember something I knew I ought to remember easily, something that ought to come clearly to mind, something just around another edge in memory. Then one day it came suddenly, peacefully. I thought, Prostitute. Get to Paris. Prostitute. I was lying in a ditch. I did not remember exactly how I had gotten there that day. It had been the first long daylight interval of fleeing, running and hiding. Paris, I

81

thought again. The underground. Prostitute will put you in touch.

I must walk, I thought. My stomach felt empty and I could feel the gauntness of my face under the stubble that covered it. I lay back in the ditch with my hands under my head and looked up at the sky. I felt very peaceful for a moment, and then the need to get on, like an old worn obsession, came again. I looked up at the first stars shining in the sky. They were still dim. I've got to take a chance, I thought. I've got to contact somebody. I watched the stars brightening. I must be near the border, I thought. But the obsession against risking capture came again, stronger, colder, than hunger. I lay there.

I woke in the sunlight, shaking with weariness and cold. The sun was rising. It warmed me. I knelt there in the ditch. I heard a noise up the road, around the curve. I crouched down in the high weeds. The sound of voices came closer. In a few moments two children appeared around the curve, coming toward me. They did not see me. I stood up and they stopped dead and stared at me, their eyes getting big.

'Where do you live?' I asked in German. They did not answer. I walked toward them a little. I pointed at the church spire across the fields.

'What town?' I asked in French. The children smiled, jabbered at each other, grinned and began laughing and pointed at my muddy and stained uniform.

'Chaumont,' one said. Then they began running.

I could not remember Chaumont on the map. I stood in the ditch and studied the map. Paris was directly west.

The sun warmed me with each step. It warmed slowly. I did not hear the truck approach from behind. The next thing there was the roar of the engine and the hiss of tires and, before I could duck into the woods on the side of the road, the truck shot past. The driver and the man beside him looked back at me over their shoulders. I waved. The truck slewed around the curve in the road and vanished. Suddenly I was tired of walking, tired of trying to escape. Again I wanted only to lie down and sleep and I could have done it without knowing. *They saw my uniform*, I thought. Then the sound of a truck came again.

I walked back into the bushes. I crouched, listening,

waiting for the truck to come into sight. I stepped out as it was almost even with me and I saw the driver, a civilian. I sprang into the middle of the road and waved my arms. The truck skidded, stopped.

The driver jerked his head out the window. He looked surprised, then suddenly scared.

'Ride?' I asked in French, jerking my thumb like an American hitchhiker. He stared at my uniform.

'How far are you going?' I asked.

The driver stared at me, his mouth opening slowly. He muttered something undistinguishable.

'How far are you going? Will you give me a ride?'

'English!' the driver shouted.

I walked toward the cab of the truck.

'Get away!' he shouted. The gears slammed into motion, ground terrifically for a fraction of an instant. The truck seemed to leap forward. I ran back into the woods and bushes.

I walked slowly in the woods, trying to follow the road. The ground rose, then I crossed an open valley and plodded beyond through a bog. I walked slowly. I knew exactly where I was going. I suddenly felt a kind of ease and peace now that I was in France and I knew where I was. I could ask here for food. It would be less of a risk. I felt suddenly fresh and light.

It was almost noon when I walked out to the highway again. I estimated I had walked about ten miles. The highway had changed; it was wide and paved now. I waited for a truck to approach with a driver in civilian clothes. This one stopped. The driver was a young man. He smiled easily, studied my uniform but looked neither surprised nor scared.

'Are you going through Chaumont?' I said.

'I'm going to Troyes. You want to go that far?' he asked.

I got in on the seat beside him.

'I want to get to Paris,' I said.

'Sit on the floor when I tell you,' he said.

The truck began to sway with speed. I did not feel anything. I thought I was hungry. I did not feel hungry. I thought I was tired. I did not feel sleepy. I woke on the floor, hearing his voice: 'Troyes.'

I got out. 'Where?'

'Back there.'

I stood in the road, rubbing my eyes. The earth was dark. The fields were all in shadow. Back in the twilight the smoke of the city hung in the setting sun, turning to rose and gold in the dying light.

'Quick now,' the driver said and switched on his lights and drove away fast. I began now to be afraid suddenly. I had been a fool to risk the main highway even though it had worked. I was afraid that out of weariness I might again take a foolish risk. And I was hungry now.

I moved into the woods again. I followed the woods along the road. Where the woods stopped a sandy road met the highway at right angles. Where the last light hung in the sky a big house rose above a grove of trees. I knelt in the ditch waiting for darkness to fall and watched the house for lights.

CHAPTER THIRTEEN

After a while a light came on in one window. Now and then the shadow of a person moved across in front of the window but I could not see whether it was a man or woman. Then the light went out.

It was cold in the brush. I began to shiver. I lay down and the ground struck coldly through my clothes. I was hungry. More hungry suddenly than I had ever been.

I watched the house for an hour; it remained dark. I had money. I could buy food. I had forgotten the money in the escape kit. Again I tried to remember what day it was but all the hours of light and darkness seemed to run together. I crept toward the house. It was a huge house. Moonlight dappled the walls and lawn. About fifty yards from the rear I stopped and watched the windows. There was neither light nor movement. The ground smelled damp and cold.

I ran to the wall of the house and rested against the cold stone. I wanted to make sure I was in the rear. I stood for several long minutes beneath a window. Then I moved along the wall, feeling for a door. It was locked. I leaned against it, listening. There was no sound inside. From the fields came the sound of crickets whirring. Then even this sound ceased and I could hear myself breathing, almost panting. I held my breath and pressed against the door again, slowly turning the knob, but it was locked. I moved and felt along the edge of the next window casement.

The window was open about two inches. I leaned against the wall until the panting stopped. Then I pushed the window open and climbed through. It was dark inside. I paused, listening. No sound, and then I smelled it. Food. My mouth began to water. I could smell it in the dark but I could see nothing.

I felt along the wall with both hands, bumped against a chair, stopped, listened. The house was silent. I put both hands flat on the table and felt slowly over the surface. The smell of food was stronger. Then I felt it, meat, cold, almost hard, but meat. I picked it up, began to eat. It was mutton. Nothing had ever tasted so delicious.

I tore another piece off the slab of mutton. The house was cold. It was so dark I could not see the meat on the plate. Then I was thirsty. I felt along the wall again, blundered against the stove, stopped. I listened. There was no sound. I went on, feeling my way past the stove, then along a bare wall. I was touching the faucet over a metal sink when I heard the noise. It was a soft sound. It was close. Somewhere a door opened. I crouched, ready to spring. The soft sound came again. I held the cold piece of mutton in my hand and held my breath tight, listening. Again a door opened. I got ready to spring.

The beam of a flashlight struck me square in the eyes, and the voice behind it was the voice of a woman. 'Stand up. Don't move or I'll kill you!'

I stood up slowly, raised my arms. A switch clicked and light flooded the room.

The woman was neither young nor old, somewhere in her late thirties. She wore jodhpurs and a sweater, and she carried the flashlight in one hand and a small automatic in the other.

'What do you want?' she asked. Her voice was cold, calm.

'I'm hungry,' I said.

'There's more in the pantry,' she said in English and gestured toward a point behind me.

85

I turned.

'Keep your hands up,' she said. Her voice was quite cold. 'Turn around.'

I stood motionless. She patted my pockets with the flashlight, keeping herself behind me and just far enough away so I couldn't turn on her.

'Sit down,' she said. There was a table and chairs. She prepared a meal in silence – bread, cheese, meat, grapes, and wine. I slumped down in the chair exhausted, feeling good for the first time in days.

'How far have you come?' she asked. She sat opposite me, the flashlight on the table, the automatic on her lap.

'Germany,' I said.

'Come here,' she said. She rose, pointed the automatic at me. Her eyes looked bright, a little mad. 'Come here.'

I stood up, walked toward her.

'Kiss me,' she said.

Her mouth was at once cold and wild with something childlike in her kiss. I felt the muzzle of the automatic against my stomach. Her arm around my shoulder was hard, mannish.

'Sit down,' she ordered. She sat opposite me again.

When I finished eating she jerked her head, gesturing for me to follow. She flashed the light ahead.

She walked behind me. We went along a dark hall with a stone floor and mounted a wide stone stairway. The light was dim. At the head of the stairway, a single lamp shone upon a pole mounted in the balustrade. Upon the wall at spaced intervals, shining faintly in the light, hung silvered wooden plaques. From each plaque hung the tail of a fox and the stairway light shone full upon the last plaque at the head of the stairs. Engraved upon the silver above the fox brush were the dates of the hunt.

It was as though in each step I saw what I must do, felt it in her presence behind me, and, thinking of it, despite fatigue and despair, felt almost at once a sense of being despoiled. I began to laugh.

'Shut up,' she said. Her voice was ice cold. 'Get in there.' A hall of darkness yawned. Ahead light shone under a door.

'Open it,' she said.

Inside, the canopied bed shadowed the dim room.

She grabbed me and flung the dead flashlight on the floor. It was like grappling with a man. Her arms were hard, but not muscled; it was as though the meager flesh upon her arms had hardened. Take her, I thought. That's what she wants. But that was not it. She wanted the struggle, as if she were going to fight me down. Later, when I thought about it, it seemed she wanted that more than the final instant of surrender. But it wasn't surrender she sought. It was the wildest coldest bedlam of desire I have ever known. Then, before the final instant, she tried to be a woman again. An anger came I had never known and I took her out of anger.

In the morning I knew it was a trick. But it didn't matter then because something else was there to think about. My clothes were gone. Upon the foot railing of the bed hung the uniform of a German captain, the trousers creased knife-sharp.

I heard her come along the hall, open the door. She stood at the foot of the bed.

'What do you want?' I said.

Her eyes were flat, cold.

'These are your clothes from now on,' she said and her voice was quiet, low. She did not look at the clothes. She looked at me lying under the canopy until I had the feeling for an instant that she was the man and I was the woman in this act.

'Put them on,' she said. 'Breakfast is served.' She still did not look at the uniform. I had the feeling she would not look at the uniform until I wore it, and later, standing in front of the mirror, the lousy taste of being despoiled, fooled, tricked, came again. I stood in rage, trying to think what to do.

She was alone downstairs, seated at a long table in a long room, her eyes bright, alert, smiling when she saw me, only she wasn't looking at me. She was watching the uniform, the way it moved or fitted or something. I could not tell. I ate. The food was hot. I wondered who else was in the house to fix such a fine breakfast: eggs, bacon, toast, butter, rolls, coffee. I'll get out of here tonight, I thought. I heard planes flying overhead, the sound drifting away.

'Get up,' she said. Then I saw the automatic. Blunt,

vicious, it lay on the table beside her hand. 'Walk around,' she said. Her voice was pleasant, almost cheery.

I got up and walked down the length of the table. I stopped in front of her.

Her eyes were faintly closed. She sat watching me.

'You will go upstairs, please.' Her voice was low, quite soft, yet with something hard in it. I did not move. She lifted the automatic slowly. Tonight, I thought, I'll get out of here tonight.

I lay all day in the room. She knocked on the door and told me lunch was on the table. That night I tried the door after dinner. It was locked. I tried the windows. They were all locked.

But she was there again in the darkness after I slept. I did not hear her slip the bolt. Her voice was tense, low. 'Fritz! Fritz! Ah!' She tore at my clothes. Her hands were hard and fierce. I stayed them, held her so she could not move.

She had turned on a table light. In the dim half-light her face and eyes were cold, almost fanatic.

'Do you realize,' she said, 'you are exactly like him?'

Her face was cold, brooding. I did not speak. I listened to her speak as if she were making some kind of recital. I looked like a German officer who had lived with her for two years. He had been sent to the Russian front. If I would stay with her I could have everything she could give me. She did not sound mad, nor even look mad. But her eyes were too bright now, and her voice too flat and cold.

'I can't stay,' I said. 'I'm on my way out.'

'You will stay or leave in that uniform.'

'If I stay, it's not unlike refusing to fight in face of the enemy. I could be court-martialed.'

'If you're caught in that German uniform, you could be shot,' she said.

'All right,' I said. 'Do you have a cigarette?'

She got up, went out, bolting the door. When she returned she had what I had counted on. I took the package of cigarettes and the box of matches.

'Anything left from dinner?' I asked.

'Wait here.'

I hated her suddenly with a fierce dread and revulsion. So I waited. I heard her bolt the door, pass along the hall.

Then I struck the first match. The curtains caught fire immediately. Then the bedspread. The smoke came too quickly. I began to choke. I hammered on the door with both fists. I heard her strike the bolt aside. The billow of smoke rushed out into the hall. For a second our faces were not a foot apart. The skin on her face was cold, dead white; her eyes were fanatical and mad again.

She struck at my head with the gun in her right hand. I struck her hard with both fists and caught her before she fell. She slumped, huddling against me, and I began to strip off her clothes. She was tall enough. Her clothes would fit. I dragged her down the hall. At the top of the stairs I had her dress off. My first impulse was simply to leave the German uniform on the floor. I threw it over the balustrade onto the floor of the main hall below. I looked at her when her eyes opened, her face shrunk in cold, wide horror. She was watching my hand. She was still watching it when the explosion from the automatic roared.

I ran, completely unaware that I was descending the staircase, completely unaware at the time that I had her dress on, knowing only a kind of desperate, childlike terror. Then I heard the sound of fire roaring above. Raising the kitchen window, I went out as I had come in and dropped down onto the soft earth and ran full speed in the dark toward the jagged crest of trees low on the horizon. In the white glare of the moon, I thought I could smell the woman burning as I ran.

I do not know how long I ran in the woods but there was faint light in the sky when I stopped. I lay under a tree and waited for the dawn. When it was almost light I saw the spire of a church sticking up above the flat country, with poplar trees standing in a long neat row along the highway beyond the woods. I walked in toward the town, keeping behind the trees.

It was a small town and where the road suddenly curved I could see down the main street. It was empty. I crossed the street. It wasn't until then that I felt the soreness of my feet. A bread shop was open on the corner. It smelled good. I was desperately hungry now. A big round-faced woman stood behind the counter. The shop was empty. I

89

looked at her and she looked at me and I grinned and shrugged.

'Can you get me clothes?' I asked. 'I have no money. I need money to get to Paris. You will be repaid.'

She did not move. Her face was motionless and her eyes dead. A cigarette stuck out of the corner of her mouth and her eyes were watery.

'What are you?'

'British flier.'

'Where did you come down?'

'East.'

'When?'

'I was captured and escaped.'

'Babe Ruth,' she said.

'What?' I asked, thinking I had misunderstood.

'Get out,' she said.

'What?' I said. The grin had helped in the beginning. I tried it again. 'I didn't hear you.'

She picked up a cup of coffee and began to drink.

'Have you got something to eat, please?'

'They're looking for you.'

'Will you give me some help, please?'

'Did you burn down her house?'

I did not say anything. Then she began to laugh. She was big and seemed to shake all over.

She filled another cup with coffee. She pushed it down the counter toward me.

'Go in back,' she said, moving her hand toward the rear of the store.

I went into the back room. It smelled of stale clothes. It was a hall with some kind of closet at the end. I sat on the single wooden chair and drank the coffee. She shut the door.

After a while she came back.

'If you need clothes,' she said, 'it will cost money.'

'I'll see that you're paid.'

'I'm sure you will. What is your name?'

I told her.

'Rank and serial number?'

You're a fool, I thought. She's either lying or peddling fliers both ways, depending on who's paying the most.

'Give your contacts my name,' I said. 'They can check.'

'You will have to stay upstairs,' she said.

I did not say anything.

When I followed her upstairs she said. 'Don't forget. You must not leave here now or you will jeopardize all of us.'

'All right.'

'I will see you have everything you need,' she said.

The room had a bed and a single window. I watched from the window all that day and all the next. At dusk on the following evening the proprietor knocked on the door and admitted a woman. She looked about thirty. Her accent was Australian. She shook my hand. She was carrying two suitcases.

'You're safe here.'

'Good.'

'I hope your feet aren't too big.'

'Do you have a full suit of clothes?'

'Everything. How do you feel?'

'Fine.'

I felt funny in the civilian clothes. The suit was my size but it seemed too big. It was loose compared to a uniform.

'Wait here,' she said. 'Don't speak to anybody who comes in. Your French is terrible.'

I smiled. 'It got me out of high school.'

'It'll keep you in France. Wait here.' She beckoned to the fat lady. They went into the back room.

When we were out on the street later she said, 'We will walk as if we are going to the railroad station.'

I said, 'What's the matter?'

'Don't talk.'

A man and woman passed.

We went on and passed the station and turned up a cobblestone street. At the edge of the town she said. 'We have to wait in the woods.'

We walked across the field. She did not speak.

'How do we get out of here?' I asked.

She looked at her watch. 'A car will be along.'

'Do many get out of the country?'

'They are checking all the trains now. Stopping them and spot checking. You can't use the trains any more.'

'Isn't driving more dangerous?'

'You can always fight and run in a car.'

'How long does it take to get across the border?'

'That depends on many things.'

'Are we going to Paris?'

'You ask a lot of questions,' she said.

'Hell, I don't even know you. For all I know you could be keeping me here until the car comes so you can turn me in.'

'Keep talking like that and you can damn well walk out of France alone.'

'I can do it.' I started to get up.

'Sit down, you bloody Yank. You don't trust your own mothers. We have to stay here until dark. There will be two cars. They will blink their lights.'

I lay back in the grass. I was very tired and after a while I fell asleep. Then a hand, a voice, roused me. I woke and heard her speaking softly. She was holding my arm tight. Through the dark I saw lights flash twice on the road.

'Let's go,' she said and sprang up. I followed her running. She was one hell of a runner. I could hardly believe she was that fast.

There were two cars. In the dark I could see the windows were rolled down on all the cars.

Somebody held the door open in the rear car and we got into the back seat. The driver turned around and smiled at us.

'Everything all right?' he asked.

'Let's go,' the woman said.

'Which way this time?'

'Bourges. St. Amand. Cerilly. St. Gervais. Mauriac. St. Santin.'

The driver got out and went up to the lead car. As he started back the lead car ground into gear and sped down the road.

Our driver got in and turned on his headlights.

'My God,' I said. 'Why don't you broadcast to the Germans that we're coming?'

'We know the roads,' she said. She laughed.

I sat back, wishing I had a gun. The car started and sped down the road at a terrific speed. There was no moonlight and the headlights were shining like car lights in peacetime. The woman sat there smiling happily. Across her legs lay a German machine gun.

It was one night two weeks later. They had dropped me from the car about a block from the café in Marseilles. They kept me in a house for two weeks. The woman's name was Gertie. I had learned that. But that was all. She seemed in charge of all the men. She gave the orders and they obeyed. So when the time came to go to Marseilles she sent me by car with two men and gave me instructions about what to say in the café.

I walked straight in and went over to the counter. It had a zinc top. I had different clothes now. A black jacket and blue workmen's trousers. And a beret. I pushed the beret on the back of my head.

The woman behind the counter looked English. She was tall and blond. She spoke French.

'Do you want coffee?' she asked.

'Hello, Gertie,' I said.

She did not appear to hear me. I had been briefed by the Australian to use another line if she did not respond to that one.

'Je cherche l'homme qui ne fume pas,' I said as carefully and clearly as I could. It was important. This woman had not been forewarned of my coming. There had not been time to send a message, Gertie had said.

'I'll serve you at the table,' she said. I was in. That was her cue. I had not missed mine.

She closed at ten o'clock. Her house was by the sea. It was a little house. There was another woman there, a Madame Clochet. She did not like my papers.

'They are too good,' she said. 'If he is picked up the police will not believe him.'

The two women sat close together in front of the fire.

'They are too perfect,' Madame Clochet said. 'I've never seen such perfect papers on an escaped prisoner.'

'He's from Gertie,' said the tall woman. She called herself Gwen. 'He's American, all right. Listen to his accent.'

'Even the Germans have some on their side.'

'Listen to him,' the woman named Gwen said again. But

suddenly her voice ceased and her gaze changed and something like fear came into her face.

She stood up and crossed the room and stood by the window and looked out. 'I know what I'm doing,' she said.

I did not move. I could feel both of them watching me. It was as if suspicion and doubt were something you could almost feel in the room like a substance. You could feel it rising between the two women.

I repeated the special words Gertie had given me. The women said nothing. They sat there watching me. I knew what they were thinking: keep him here and double check, only by the time word comes back from Gertie the Germans might close in. Or get rid of him. I would have to call the turn now.

'O.K.' I said. 'I'll get out.' I got up.

She walked over from the window. She looked straight up into my face.

'How do you expect to get over?'

'I know how the country lies,' I said. 'Don't worry about me.'

I started toward the door.

'You're crazy,' she said. 'You'll have to get out tonight. The frontier's tight. You'll never make it that way.'

'What other way is there?'

'They're watching the frontier. We've had too much luck there.'

I did not say anything.

'You follow the coast,' she said. 'Go down the coast.' She named the towns and the cliff to cross. 'Then go to the Bar de la Marney. It's in the Rue Fresselines.'

'Who do I ask for?'

She smiled.

'Ned Axt,' she said. 'There is only one man behind the counter. He sleeps above the bistro.'

'How far is it?'

'Ten kilometers. He'll give you new papers. Get rid of these. They are too perfect.'

'How do I get across?'

'He will get you a job on the crew. Don't take these papers. Go to the Rue de la Sphynx in Casablanca. Number 43. Ask for Peter. He's English. He'll get you through to Lisbon. I don't know why I doubt you. But they didn't warn us.'

'Perhaps there's too much heat up north. No time.'

'Perhaps,' she said. 'The secret police are every place. You must leave tonight.'

She opened the door.

'I'll take him to the path at Cuino,' she said to Madame Clochet. Madame Clochet said nothing.

The stars were out. We walked far from the house. The path mounted steadily. From below came the sound of the sea. It sounded hollow and distant. She stopped and caught my hand.

'Please do me a favor?' she asked.

'I'll send you a postcard.'

'Listen,' she said. 'I would help more. But Clochet makes the decisions. Do you know the squadron at Tangmere?'

'I'm on bombers.'

'Do you know Tangmere?'

'Of course.'

'My husband is there. Tell him . . . tell him, I'm fine. Please. Squadron Leader Doyle.'

'You bet.'

'Good luck. Have a good walk,' she said.

CHAPTER FOURTEEN

It was strange seeing London again. I had not been away long but now everything in London looked smaller, even Big Ben and Piccadilly Circus. I had been gone only a few weeks but somehow I felt much older. And all the distances somehow looked different. I could not understand the feeling. I was tired, too.

I came out of the hotel and stood on the sidewalk. It was a beautiful sunny morning, but I couldn't relax. I felt nervous and restless.

Then I saw Joan coming up the street. She was walking, carrying her bag. She was wearing a uniform, but even in that her figure was unmistakable, and even at that distance I felt her loveliness, and felt lust and love and tenderness all at once, together. I had never before felt all these things for one person.

I walked down the street to meet her. I kissed her standing on the corner while she complained that peo)le were staring at us.

'Let 'em look,' I said.

'Darling, you're choking me,' she said.

'God, you look wonderful.'

'How do you feel?'

'Perfect. Here. Give me your bag.'

I took her bag and we walked back along the street to the hotel.

'How long do you have, darling?' she asked.

'Ten days. What about you?'

'Seven days.'

An expression I could not understand passed over her face.

'Wonderful,' she said. We walked up the steps into the hotel foyer.

Joan had reserved a front room for herself. She sat on the corner of her bed and I kissed her and held her until the waiter brought the drinks up.

'What should we do?' I asked. 'You're the boss.'

'Whatever you feel like.'

'I wish we could stay right in this room for ten days,' I said.

'You expect too much.'

'Drink up. I'm two drinks ahead of you.'

'I hope nothing happens,' she said. She looked sad suddenly.

'What are you talking about?'

'You never know in this business.'

'You do have seven days?'

'Yes.'

'Is there anything they might call you on?'

'That's it. I never know.'

'Well, don't think about it.'

'I'll try catching up with you. Ring for the waiter, will you, darling?'

I called for two more highballs and sat down beside her. I still felt uneasy, though I had kissed her. I did not know why. I suppose it was because I was more in love with her

96

now. I knew now how much I had missed her. I smelled her hair. It smelled soft and sweet. I wanted to kiss her again, but there was a strange edge of shyness between us. I knew it would pass and somehow it seemed a part of this time of bliss and leisure we would share.

'Where's your room?' she asked.

'Just down the hall.'

'Darling, would you excuse me while I unpack and freshen up?'

'Dismissed?'

'Out you go.'

'Joan, let's get married.'

'Out you go.'

But I didn't get out. I stayed and helped her unpack. I had been in rooms with her before but this was different and we both sensed it and she knew I was watching her as she moved around the room. I had the feeling we were married and this was our first day together.

'Come here,' I said. But she did not move. She was bending over the bureau, closing the drawer.

'What's the matter?' I asked.

She straightened up and looked at me.

She smiled, 'I don't know. I feel like a silly schoolgirl somehow. I don't know why.'

'I know,' I said. I walked over and took her in my arms and held her there and kissed her. I could feel her begin to relax. I could feel myself begin to relax. It was suddenly as if we were a little the people we had been when we first met, only now kissing her was even better, as if somehow we were better people, though I could not understand why.

But somehow I wanted to delay making love to her. I wanted her nakedness and I knew she wanted mine but I did not want to rush it now that I had her here. We had days ahead.

But I kissed her again and felt her heart beating and began to feel everything, the tension, the strain, the weeks of worry, slip away in her arms. Yet somehow I felt she sensed my waiting feeling. She lay lightly in my arms. I stopped kissing her.

'What're you thinking?' she asked.

'Two weeks,' I said. 'We've got two whole weeks.'

'Not quite.'

'I'm marking it that way.'

'What happened to Cuddington?' she asked.

'I don't know.'

'What happened after the crash?'

So I told her the whole story, from take-off to capture and escape along the coast and over the mountains into Spain.

'How did you manage to get out of jail in Spain?' she asked.

'The consul finally turned up.'

Then I kissed her again and wanted her again and still did not want to rush it. I wanted to wait until darkness. Somehow it would be even better then.

She drew back and then stood up as if catching her breath.

'Come on,' she said, smiling. 'Let's look at the town.'

I was relieved. It was as though she sensed exactly how I felt and that she felt the same way.

'It looks different all right,' I said. 'Everything looks smaller.'

'You look the same,' she said and leaned over. I kissed her again. 'One moment,' she said. 'I'll fix my hair.'

I lifted the blackout curtain and looked out. Joan and I had had a good dinner at the Mirabelle. Now we were back in her room. The moon was shining on the street below. Hell of a night for night fighters. I was glad I wasn't going out tonight. A good night to get silhouetted against that naked, white full moon. I drew the blackout curtain, snapped on the light.

I lay back in a chair. I listened to the shower in the bathroom.

'Darling,' she called, 'bring me a cigarette while I dry off.'

I did not move. I was back where I had been before earlier in the evening. It was as if we had first met. I wanted her alone in the darkness.

'There,' she called. 'I turned the shower off. Can you hear me?'

'Receiving.'

'Cigarette?'

'Come in.'

'Cigarette? she called.

I did not answer. She burst into the room. She had lovely broad creamy shoulders and fine big arms. Her breasts and shoulders and long hair were made for love. Her flesh glowed warmly in the light. I stood up. Even from across the room I could feel her tenderness. I walked toward her.

'Were you hit there?' she asked, surprised.

I nodded. It was not fit to remember now. I did not want to remember it. None of that old dead hour of dread was fit now.

'What was it?' she asked. 'Flak?'

'No. Cannon shell.'

'Darling, it was much too close.'

That night came there now. I hated it. It did not belong here in this room, in this warmth and light. It was another world I wanted far away. It was intruding. It had no right. She looked down at my leg. In the door mirror behind her I saw my thigh muscle bulge in the light and the two concave white wedge-shaped scars.

'When did that happen?' she asked.

'I had it before. We got hit over Kiel.'

There were no scars on her clear white smooth thighs.

'Oh, God,' I said suddenly. 'Let's get married.'

'I can't,' she said.

'But if you did you'd be out of the service. Right?'

'Would you do it that way? Yourself?'

'You deserve it. You've done enough for a woman in this war.'

She shook her head. 'Who has?'

'You,' I said and walked past her into the bathroom.

'All right,' she said. 'Let me ask. Are you going back on ops?'

'Yes.'

'See what I mean?'

'No.'

'You just refuse to, that's all,' she said.

'I might not,' I said. 'They might not okay me for ops.'

'I should think not after that last show.'

I turned on the shower and got out after a minute or two. I stood there drying myself.

'Are you really?' she asked.

'What?'

'Going back on ops?'

'I don't know.'

'Will they make you?'

'Not for a while.' I knew I could get back on if I asked for it. Usually if you escaped you didn't have to go back on ops again, but you could do it if you asked. I was afraid I would ask and I was afraid I would not, because I knew what would happen if I didn't. The first couple of nights I would hear the engines going over, bound for Germany, and I would be relieved, thankful that I didn't have to go, and then the old illusion of being invulnerable would return again and with it a sense of longing compounded of shame for not being up there with them. It's a piece of cake, I would think, hearing the engines running up for the night's mission, wishing I were with them. So it was best to go directly on ops again and finish the tour.

'How about you?' I asked.

'I was thinking,' she said. Then: 'If you would quit . . . no, I can't do that.'

'Why not?'

'If you would promise . . .'

'Look, I'll finish up this tour and we'll get married and I'll get you pregnant. Then they'll have to discharge you.'

'You don't understand.'

'I understand I love you and want to marry you and you've done enough,' I said.

'Are you so sure?'

'Stop being so damned brave,' I said.

'This war is a game, a lark, an adventure to you.'

'Maybe, but it's my skin, too.'

'Oh, darling, come here.'

The sound of her voice saddened me. I wanted her out of the forces. I wanted her safe. It was not easy for me to understand her sense of duty. Maybe I was selfish in not understanding. She had seen things in France I had never seen. I went into the bedroom.

'Forget it,' I said. 'It'll work out.'

'Come here,' she said. Her body was incredibly soft. I kissed her shoulders and breasts and then her mouth and held her close and drew her up to me.

It was a night I shall never forget, our minds and bodies drowning, floating, the soft clamor of blood in our ears.

The room seemed to dissolve, while our flesh touched softly, softly flowed through a warm, glowing light. Our bodies were like flowers suddenly. We lay lightly on cool water, our limbs flowing into a cool gloom of shadow, flowing far away upon an immensity of water, tranquil shores receding further and further. Then a murmur came, rushing, rushing, rushing.

'Oh, darling, darling,' she cried. I felt her subtle muscles arch, cry. My mind disintegrated, and in the dark upon the water, swiftly, gently, like flowers, we rose, furious, supple and flexing. Our mouths were warm as rain, softer, softer, and then the water slowly azure again beneath warm stars, the naked muscles reclining laxly, golden, humming, at ease.

'Oh, God,' she cried in soft and astonished ecstasy.

We woke later, touching each other. The warmth and glow of our bodies was like a drug, at once tender and exhilarated, trembling again with delight, sighing, entranced.

Her love and warmth came suddenly in a rushing curve through my body, her breasts swollen with love, pressing, pressing, and again tender fullness, rising and rising. There was no sound, suddenly no light, no motion in the world; then only our nerves trembling gratefully, holding enraptured into ourselves, our souls and mind.

I kissed her shoulder, held her close. Again we slept.

A sound, far-faint, then abruptly peremptory, roused me. I rolled over in bed. The phone was ringing. I got out of bed, crossed the room and picked up the phone.

'Hello,' said a man's voice I did not know. 'Is Miss DeMarney there?'

'What do you want?'

'Please tell her Jay is calling.'

'What is it?' Joan called from across the room.

'I don't know,' I said. Then: 'What the—'

'Flight Lieutenant O'Hara,' the voice began.

She took the phone out of my hand. She put it against her ear.

'Yes,' she said. 'Yes, I can talk. Go ahead . . . Yes, Jay . . .' She slanted her head, listening. 'I told you we would be right here . . . Right. I'll see you at the office.' She hung the phone up slowly. She stood there thoughtfully.

'I'll be a—' I started to say.

'It's like being shot,' she said.

'What?'

'He promised,' she said.

'Who is he?'

Suddenly her eyes flooded with tears. I held her against me, sensing the truth.

'What's wrong, Joan?'

'God must be a very angry man today.'

'That was the office, wasn't it?'

'I have to go back, Jack.'

'When?'

'This morning.'

'My God!'

'This is a lovely room, darling,' she said, blinking, swallowing. 'Did you have a good sleep?'

'I slept like a log.'

'Let's get dressed and order some breakfast.'

'What's up?' I asked.

'I don't know.'

'Ops?'

'I don't know, darling,' she said.

'They can call you just like that?'

She smiled, snapped her fingers.

I had the feeling she knew what she had to do at the office.

'When can you get away?' I asked.

'I can't.'

'What time is it?'

'Nine-thirty.' I reached for the phone, ordered breakfast. We were tired. I was worried about her too. Too tired and worried now for love. It was all over. We had called off the war and they had called the war on again. I put my arms around her, but she seemed far away from me suddenly, quite changed, another person thinking about what she must do, taking stock of some other situation.

'I love you,' I said.

'I love you too, darling.'

I felt a cold hard ball of fear in my stomach.

While we were eating breakfast I said, 'What time do you have to be at the office?'

'Any time this morning.'

'Then you're not on tonight?'

'I may not be on at all.'

'Why don't I wait here then?'

'No good, darling,' she said.

'Then he told you?'

She smiled.

'What?'

'Where they're dropping you?'

'Even if they had, I couldn't tell you. Eat your eggs. They're delicious.'

I did not move. I felt dead inside.

'Can you give me a call tonight?' I asked.

'Darling, I'll call you tomorrow.'

I had the feeling she was lying. She would be gone tonight, dropped some place on the continent.

'All right,' I said. 'I suppose I might as well head back to the squadron.'

'Afraid so.'

Then suddenly she began to cry. She dropped her fork. I had never seen her sob like this before. She had been in command of herself. I put my arm around her and held her tight.

'Don't cry,' I said. 'Please don't.'

She blinked her eyes and tried to stop but she couldn't and she leaned against me crying for what seemed a long while. At last I felt her shoulders and face quiet and she whispered, 'Don't you go on ops, please.'

'All right.'

'Promise?'

'Promise.'

'I'd die if anything happened to you, Jack.'

'What about you?'

'I'll be all right,' she said. 'These drops are a piece of cake now.'

'Haven't you any idea when you'll be doing it?'

She shook her head.

'I won't go near an airplane till I hear from you,' I said.

She dressed and packed in silence. I ordered up a couple of drinks. They were a help but they really didn't do anything. When I looked at my watch again it was ten-thirty.

'Don't come down,' she said.

We kissed gently. She stood there for a moment, then stepped away.

'Be careful, Jack.'

I laughed. 'You should be telling me that?'

She kissed me. I opened the door and picked up her single bag.

'I'll come down,' I said.

'No. Good-bye, love. I'll phone you tomorrow.'

'Be careful, darling,' I said.

She stepped out into the hall, reached back and took the bag from my hand and walked down the hall to the elevator. I heard the elevator coming up the shaft. I did not shut the door until after I heard her get on and the elevator descending. Then I shut the door and stood in the room alone.

CHAPTER FIFTEEN

I rode out from the station in a taxi across the Yorkshire moors to the airfield. I did not have the feeling as I had had before of going back to the old squadron. It looked somehow strange, almost unfamiliar. It was almost evening and across the field they were running up the engines for that night's attack. I thought of Joan and Cuddington and wondered if they would be dead together in the morning. I did not know why but I felt then that Cuddington was dead. It was not until after the war that I heard he was never found, not even the grave-registration teams found a trace of him.

I walked along the road to squadron headquarters and checked in with the adjutant.

'Well, Jack,' he said, smiling. He got up from behind his desk and we shook hands.

'How was Spain?' he asked.

'Sunny. Send me back.'

'The skipper was just here. There's a do on. He's going.'

'Where?'

'Lorient. You're in Hut 7, Room 4.'

'Fine. Come on over to the mess. I'll buy you a drink before dinner.'

'Righto, Jack. Nice to have you back.'

The Nissen huts were dispersed about the field. I walked along between the machine shop and aircraft-repair hangars and along the path to the Nissen hut site. I walked down the hall of the hut to Room 4. The door was open. I went in and found a young pilot officer lying on one cot reading a copy of *News of the World*.

'Hello,' he said and sat up and smiled. He looked no older than nineteen. 'I'm Peter Wyeth.' He looked even younger when I got close to him. His cheeks were pink against his fair skin and his hair was blond.

'I'm Jack O'Hara,' I said. 'The adjutant sent me over.' I dropped my kit bag on the floor.

'I came in yesterday,' he said. 'This your first day?'

I hung my tunic over the back of a chair and sat down on the other cot.

'I used to be with the squadron,' I said. 'I've been on leave.'

'Oh.' I saw his eyes go suddenly to the row of ribbons on my tunic.

I had the feeling suddenly I somehow didn't deserve the medals. I wondered how I had ever received them when I had been so worried about flying again. They seemed out of place suddenly. Was everybody as scared as I had been at times? Come on, I thought, you were like this after the last crash and it went away once you got that stick in your hands again.

Looking at him I felt older and somehow dried up.

'Where did you do O.T.U.?' I asked. I began to open my kit bag.

'Abingdon.'

'Whitleys?' I asked.

'Right.'

'Where did you convert onto four engines?'

'Riccal,' he said.

'Isn't that near Selby?'

He laughed. 'A few pubs in that town, aren't there?'

I remembered Selby. Thirty-two pubs. One lovely cathedral.

105

'You haven't done any ops then?' I asked.

'At O.T.U. we dropped leaflets on Calais,' he said awkwardly.

'That can be rough enough there,' I said, not wanting to frighten him. You had to gun-break them easy as you would a bird dog. But what if the poor kid got sent to the Ruhr the first mission over? The fast break-in. If he survived, it surely wouldn't build his confidence.

I looked at my watch. 'Had dinner?' I asked.

'Just going up,' he said.

'Let's go,' I said.

The next morning I walked over to the wing commander's office. He sat at his desk with maps on the wall and typed sheets of paper on the desk.

'Well,' he said, 'how are you, Jack?'

'I'm okay.'

'Good.'

'How's the squadron been doing?'

'The odds seem to be swinging our way more and more.'

'What are losses?'

'Oh, three per cent. Maybe a little more.'

'Not bad.'

'The Americans have been a help,' said the wing commander. He smiled and offered me a cigarette. 'Their claims on Jerry fighters are fantastic. American air gunners must all be Daniel Boone's direct descendants. However, if only fifty per cent of their claims are correct, it's a big help.'

'How do they find the weather?' I lit the cigarette from the lighter on his desk.

'They've learned precision bombing in daylight is a bit difficult in European weather.'

'What about the Krupp works?'

'About seventy per cent of the built-up area around the plants of Essen has been knocked out.'

'Any more talk of invasion?'

'Lots of talk.'

'How long do you think it'll be?'

The wing commander shrugged. 'It won't be too long.'

'What's the German fighter strength?'

'About three thousand first line. A lot of new night fighters have been brought in from the Russian front.'

'You depress me,' I said.

'How many missions do you need to finish your tour?'

'About ten.'

'This your third tour?' he asked.

'That's right.'

'How would you like to instruct? Right here in the squadron?'

I did not say anything. I did not look at him. I could feel him watching me. I looked at my hand snubbing out the cigarette butt in the ash tray. My hand was steady, but this did not mean anything. I did not want to do the remaining missions. I did not want anybody to know I was scared and I didn't think it showed.

'I need somebody with all these new kids they're sending us,' the wing commander said.

'Oh, hell,' I said, 'I'd just as soon finish up and have the tour completely out of the way.'

'I hoped you might see it our way.'

'Ten missions shouldn't take too long.'

'Listen, Jack, I don't believe you're ready for the kind of operations we're flying now. Almost all of them are deep penetration. The Jerries light up the bomber stream with flares twenty miles from the target. It's like a daylight raid only you won't have any fighter protection or any formation cross fire.'

'It can always be worse.'

'Well, I'm going to give you a couple of milk runs first, Jack. Get your hand in again.'

I did not say anything because I was grateful.

'Give "William" a test flight today and I'll put you on tonight,' he said.

'Okay,' I said. I saluted him.

'Take Cunningham's crew,' he said. 'They've done about twenty ops. Good lads.'

'Right,' I said.

It was a long day. I flew the test hop that morning, up to the Wash and back. I waited the rest of the afternoon in the mess for Joan to call. I did not hear from her.

CHAPTER SIXTEEN

The sun was going down when the wing commander came into the mess. I was sitting there listening to the radio and drinking a glass of beer, but not really tasting the beer nor hearing the radio. The wing commander beckoned to me and I went over to the door.

'Briefing in half an hour,' he said. I felt my heart kick over. Other members of the air crew did not move nor look up. It was to be a stand down for the squadron tonight. I went back into the room and told each member of my crew to be ready for briefing in half an hour. They rose slowly, putting away their newspapers and magazines.

'What's the scoop?' asked the navigator.

'Probably a leaflet drop,' I told him.

The wing commander stood on the dais at the end of the Nissen hut used for briefing. On the wall behind him was a map with a red ribbon on it stretching from England to St. Martial on the river Dordogne in southern France. The wing commander suddenly looked older to me. His voice was sharp.

'Gentlemen! We have a special show for you tonight.' He paused and looked down at us. 'You haven't done this type of thing before. Here's Intelligence and we'll let them tell you about it.'

I heard the door open at the rear of the Nissen hut and the sound of feet coming along the wall toward the dais. There were two men, one in RAF blue and one in the dark blue of the Free French Air Force, and then a woman. I saw her face, but it seemed suddenly meaningless, touching my mind like a passing strange snapshot. It was Joan. I watched her walk to the dais. She did not see me. She sat down on a chair beside a table under the wall map. She stared straight ahead as if looking beyond our faces. I felt cold in my guts.

'You're to drop an agent tonight,' the intelligence officer said.

I listened to his instructions and memorized them! Time

of drop, height, location of signal fires. His words sounded far-off, tapping against the top of my mind.

'Any questions?'

Nobody spoke. This was a piece of cake compared to running in on a flak-defended target. I imagine the crew going with me was grateful, an easy mission like this to mark up in their log books on the road to finishing a tour, one more mission closer to being taken off ops to instruct.

'Well, good luck!' We set our watches. Take-off in an hour. There would be just time to change into flying togs after operational tea, then run up engines before take-off.

The rest of the crew went back to the mess. The intelligence officer was rolling up his map. The wing commander was talking to Joan, standing in front of her so she did not see me walk up to the platform. I felt my mouth growing dry and there was the cold empty feeling deepening in my guts. I was conscious of my hands, sticky with sweat.

'Hello, Joan,' I said.

She looked up and greeted me. I stood in front of her.

'So you know each other?' the wing commander said. 'Well, well, Jack's your pilot tonight.'

'Yes,' she said, her eyes motionless, resting lightly on nothing at all. 'We met in London at a party.'

'Oh, really?' said the wing commander. 'Well, you're in good hands. Won't you join us in the mess for tea?' He glanced at his watch. 'Plenty of time.'

As she rose I heard her suck in her breath through her teeth.

Tomorrow, I thought, we will each of us wake into different worlds.

Outside it was raining faintly in the darkness. The night seemed to lay over everything, patient and quiet, waiting.

In the mess there was a terrific party going on. Everybody was making a great deal of noise, celebrating a stand down on ops for two nights and this was the first night. The girls were from town and they looked excited and working hard to be cheerful. It sounded as if everybody were singing and whistling.

The wing commander excused himself and went into the party and Joan and I went into the mess. Songs roared on from the bar-room.

'How are you, darling?' she said. She squeezed my hand under the table as the waitress brought us tea and eggs and spam.

'My God,' I said.

'I'll be back in a week.'

'What're you going for?'

'I'm taking money in and instructions to the underground.'

'When will you be back?'

'Fortnight.'

'Will they shoot you if you get caught?'

'Perhaps. Perhaps not. Usually there's long, long questioning. Darling, I'm not important enough for them to shoot.'

'You're crazy to go on pulling these trips.'

'Don't tell me about that. Tell me, what did you do after I left?'

'I came back to the squadron.'

'Do you have to go back on ops so soon?'

'This is a piece of cake. A warm-up.'

The tea was getting cold and the eggs were cold when I ate them. The rain fell steadily against the window.

'More tea?' I asked.

She shook her head. I looked at my watch.

'Come on,' I said. 'I'll give you a ride down to the line.'

The bus was outside standing in the rain and we got in. We were the first ones in the bus. I sat there, conscious of the sweetness of her, remembering my fingers on her smooth white shoulders, her red mouth on mine, and her breasts against me. I kissed her, holding her tight. I felt strengthened somehow and I hoped I was giving her the same feeling.

She drew back her head, looked at me. 'Well, sweet?' she said.

I nodded and smiled. 'You look competent as hell, darling.'

'I hope you're a good pilot.'

'I don't even feel like one now.'

Just then the rear door of the bus opened and the crew climbed in.

It was raining hard as we walked from the bus to the aircraft, and the rain was cold and the sky was black. The

110

crew chief came down out of the cockpit and we stood under the wing.

'Bloody weather, sir.'

'See you at breakfast, Mac.'

The crew climbed into the fuselage and I stood there with Joan until we were alone. 'I hope this front clears up before we hit the coast. I'm going in high across the coast if we have any cloud cover at all. Otherwise we'll stay on the deck.'

'Have you ever flown south of France before?' she asked.

'On the way to Milan and Turin. Not quite as far west as we're going.'

'Some nice hills.'

'Good-bye, darling,' I said and kissed her quickly.

I started walking toward the door in the fuselage and she caught my shoulder and I turned and kissed her once more.

'Come on,' I said. 'We'll be late.'

I helped her climb inside. I wondered what kind of a reception we'd have waiting for us over there. Well, one thing, we weren't carrying any bomb load so we could go in fast. I climbed up into the cockpit. I left her sitting on the floor beside the navigator's table. She looked different, strange, in the flying suit, with the chest-pack parachute sitting on her lap.

I started the engines and the motors stuttered into life, rocking the plane on the hard stand. Then the engines began to fire evenly. I throttled down, running the engines quietly. Outside I could see the little tongues of flame flickering out of the exhausts.

I adjusted the rudder pedals, set the compass and plugged in my intercom. I started to rev up the engines. This was going to be the most careful cockpit check I had ever made.

I checked revolutions, temperatures and boost pressure carefully. The noise of the engines rose, shutting out the world. I listened closely to each engine, switching off each circuit of the ignition system in turn. Again, as on many nights before, I felt as if I were becoming part of the machine. Finally everything looked and sounded right.

I snapped the oxygen mask and microphone across my face, fastening it hard against the side of my helmet.

'Pilot to navigator! Give me first course.'

'One-seven-two magnetic.'

'One-seven-two magnetic,' I repeated back. 'Thanks. Hello, sparks,' I called to the radio operator. 'Everything jake?'

'Righto, sir.'

I checked the tail gunner and bombardier in the nose turret. I switched off the cockpit lights. I taxied slowly out and around the perimeter track to the mouth of the runway. A green flare from the tower told me it was time to take off. I pumped on flap, put the props in fine pitch. I held the brakes on hard, opened the throttles slowly, then let the brakes off. The plane moved swiftly along the runway through the rain and darkness.

The flares on each side of the runway fled backward, flashing yellow in the rain. I pushed the heavy wheel forward. We were going fast now, the last flare fleeing away behind us. Then the plane felt just right. I eased the wheel back. The machine bumped once and began to climb into the rain.

I quickly checked the engine revolutions and air speed. Yes, we were climbing straight and level. I pumped off flap, throttled down, put the air screws into coarse pitch.

At three thousand feet I turned onto course. The blinking, fading necklace of lights marking the airfield fell away into the dark emptiness of the sky and the cockpit felt as it had felt on so many nights, like a small room, the stars rising out of the darkness as we broke through clouds.

We crossed the coast just south of Folkestone, sliding along in the darkness, the engines roaring steadily. I held the plane steady on course, checking the instrument panel and calling the flight engineer on the intercom from time to time.

In the middle of the English Channel we reached fourteen thousand feet, and ahead and behind searchlights swung in smooth, searching arcs, from the coast of France and the cliffs of Dover.

I turned south on a new course, heading toward the Channel Islands, holding now the semblance of Joan in my mind.

Ahead rose a tremendous mass of white clouds, towering and cold. It was too high to climb over and we went in, the plane pitching and rolling on the rising currents. I pushed the throttles open and we began to climb and a few minutes later we droned on through clear darkness.

'Hello, pilot. Radio operator here.'

'Hello, sparks.'

'There's a bandit in the area.'

'Where are we, navigator?' I asked.

'Eleven-zero-zero-zero, flying a little southeast of Dungeness.'

'What do they say at base?'

'One bandit in area.'

'We'll go down a bit?'

I dived. It was bumpy. We picked up speed. The night fighter wouldn't have our range. I told the navigator I was changing course every three minutes, with a change in altitude every two minutes. I flew on dead-reckoning for ten minutes and then asked the radio operator to get us a fix. The fix came and I began to climb again.

'What does base say?' I asked. 'Bandit still following?'

'He's gone home,' the radio operator replied cheerfully.

It was a good night for a night fighter. There was no moon against which our turret gunners could see them approaching, and if they came up underneath us they could see our dark shape against the lighter darkness of the sky's dome.

After a while the navigator said, 'Ten minutes to the coast.' I had the old feeling again, cold guts, teeth chattering a little, wishing we were running in on the target. *Come on, come on,* I told myself. *This is a piece of cake. A drop. No flak on this target.*

The navigator called out that we had crossed the coast and gave a new heading south. Sometimes far down I saw lights flashing, single lights, perhaps bikes, and once a flashlight blinking the Morse code V for victory.

Suddenly the sky filled with antiaircraft fire. Round balls of smoke with an orange flash in the center burst uncomfortably close.

'Hey, navigator,' I said. 'Sure you got the right course?'

He did not answer. I called to the gunners to watch for fighters. The flak might only be a signal to night fighters that we were in the area. A burst of flak off the starboard wing made the plane rock and I dived and climbed, looking ahead suddenly at a cone of searchlights, wondering where the night fighters were lurking to pick us up.

Soon we were out of range of the lights and flak batteries.

'Starboard, low,' said one of the gunners. 'Get ready to turn. Fighter!'

'Turn starboard!' the tail gunner called. I kicked hard on the rudder and pushed the wheel forward. As the machine dived and turned, two long threads of fire passed over the top of the cockpit.

'He's got a friend!' called the top turret gunner. 'Attacking port. High! Turn!'

I had corkscrewed left and was climbing now in the opposite direction. It was only a matter of shoving the nose down and turning in the same direction. In the darkness, against the faint starlight, small round flashes of fire streaked across in front of our nose. The top gunner cursed and I kicked on the opposite rudder.

I heard our guns rattling, then a jubilant voice.

'Got him! Got him!'

'Okay. Watch it!'

The top turret gunner reported another fighter. 'Twin engine. Starboard beam. He's flashing a green light.'

I knew the trick. It was a good one and we were goners if it worked. The green light was a signal for a simultaneous attack, one fighter coming in dead astern while the other made a full beam attack. That way, if they timed themselves right, one of them would have a clear shot at you no matter how tight a turn you held.

I dived starboard, my hands wet inside my gloves. I was frightened. I pulled the wheel back hard.

'Missed us,' the tail gunner called.

'Watch dead astern low,' I said. We came out of the turn. That would bring the rear fighter directly behind and a little below the tail of our plane.

I looked ahead for a cloud. Only darkness and stars. I rammed the wheel forward. The wheel began to feel limp in my hands. My arms and shoulders and body felt weak. *Come on, come on*, I thought, *fly this bastard, fly it. Keep flying it.* I heard the flight engineer screaming the air speed was close to three hundred. I could not seem to see.

I pulled on the wheel. I could gradually see again. I got the aircraft level.

'They must've run out of ammo,' the tail gunner reported. 'They're gone.'

'Up a little,' the navigator said. 'You're pretty low. There's plenty of hill around here.'

I felt like whistling suddenly. My teeth were chattering.

We gained height and got a new fix and set course and then flew on, mile after mile over southern France, gradually losing height. We flew at two thousand feet over the dark countryside.

'Fifteen minutes to drop,' the navigator reported. I felt half awake, as if in a dream, frightened that perhaps it was real.

'Watch for the fires,' I heard my voice saying, to the gunners.

Oh, God, I thought suddenly, seeing in my mind her face, tense and white as she stood ready above the open bomb-bay doors. *Let her live*, I thought. *Let her live and come back. Let her come back. I'll be good to her the rest of my life. Just let her live . . . just let her live . . . just let us have that happiness.*

At fifteen hundred feet I saw some lights on the ground off to starboard and turned toward them, opening up the engines.

'Seven minutes,' the navigator called. 'Action stations.'

Faraway to the southwest a long string of light flak bursts went up, turning and twisting.

'Three minutes . . . opening bomb doors.'

Then I saw brilliant but small flashes of gunfire on the ground. Then north of the flashes a series of fires, triangular in shape, lit up the countryside, as if somebody had abruptly ignited gasoline tins.

'Joan,' I said.

I knew she was plugged in with headphones listening to the navigator call off the minutes.

'One minute . . .' Then the navigator began calling the seconds: 'Six . . . five . . . four . . . three . . . two . . .'

'Joan,' I said.

'Go!' the navigator shouted.

'Be careful, Jack,' she called, and that was all. I throttled back as the seconds counted off and the navigator shouted, 'Jump!' Then I saw the burst of light flak again and saw a gun flash nearby, shooting at us.

'Damn it!' I said, and rammed the throttles forward and kicked the nose up and around in a bank. For an instant the plane seemed to fall sideways and then it pulled out. I hauled back on the wheel and felt the controls losing effect, heard my voice panting. The plane seemed to stand on its tail; then very slowly it began to gain height. I sat crouched over the wheel, panting like an animal.

Then the engines picked up power. It was bumpy. I checked the oil temperatures, which I thought might be rising, but they were perfect on both starboard and port engines. We flew on, climbing toward high clouds. My eyes were tired and my legs and arms felt stiff.

Suddenly there was a terrific noise under the port engines. The boost needle shot up from minus two to zero. The revolution counter sagged. I slammed the throttle back, rammed on the left rudder to hold the course.

'What the hell?' the navigator bawled.

'The supercharger's hit,' I said. 'Port engines are almost gone.' I opened the starboard engines to hold height.

'How long to the coast?' I asked.

'Hour and a half.'

I looked at the oil temperature.

'She won't hold up,' I said. 'She's doing everything she can do right now.'

Just then the inner port engine burst an oil pipe. The oil splashed against the cockpit window. I held the wheel hard. We were flying at five thousand feet and all around us was the hilly, wild country of southern France. The plane held level, sinking steadily.

'Bail out!' I yelled. 'Bail out!'

The crew called out their positions, each in turn, just before bailing out. When I was sure they were all gone I got the plane to come around in a slow circle. I had the throttles wide open on the starboard engines, keeping on bottom rudder, but the nose was still dropping. This was too damn dangerous. I should have gotten out with the crew, but I wanted to get out near the dropping point.

The air speed had dropped to one hundred and twenty.

The wheel felt loose in my hand. Suddenly the port wing went down. Fear surged up in a great wave in my stomach. I heard myself curse the plane in a thin voice. I gave the starboard engines another burst and the port wing came up a little.

I felt suddenly cool, though scared. I pulled my feet off the rudder pedals. I unlocked my Sutton harness. The ground was too damn near now.

I grabbed the top of the wheel with one hand and pushed the hatch door open overhead. I stood up on the seat. I had the terrible sickening feeling I was not moving quickly enough.

Christ! I thought. *To die, trapped in here.* Time seemed without any reality. I clutched the top of the open hatch and pushed upwards with both hands and felt the wind hurl me suddenly outwards and over the side. I felt a sharp blow on the shoulder.

Then I was falling. It was horrible because I seemed to have time to think about it. I was so scared I felt a kind of crazy elation. I counted five to get clear of the falling aircraft. Then I jerked at the rip cord. An eternity seemed to pass. *Damn . . . I was too close . . . it won't open in time.*

Abruptly the harness jerked and I found myself sitting. I felt myself swinging gently back and forth. As I looked to the south the aircraft turned slowly over on one wing in a shower of sparks and dived into the ground. Flames shot upwards.

The darkness was silent but to the south the ground was lit with gun flashes though there were no corresponding flashes in the sky. Was there a battle or skirmish on? I heard the rattle of machine-gun fire, explosions of mortars.

I struck the ground heavily, fell forward, and was dragged nearly a block before I could empty the air out of the canopy. I stripped off the harness. The field was plowed, dark and silent. I gathered the canopy and squatted, listening. The gun-fire was faint, still to the south. I had a splitting headache.

I don't think I was fully conscious of what I was doing. I began to walk across the plowed field. I fell several times. I heard my voice saying something but I could not understand the words.

I began to feel a wind blowing. The thing to do was to

find trees and hide the parachute. I could not see the landscape but suddenly the plowed field ceased and I stumbled and fell against a pile of brush. I felt inside the brush pile in the dark. I knew I was up on some kind of ridge. The thing to do was to sit tight until dawn. Hide and keep warm. I pushed up and under the pile of brush and shoved the parachute canopy inside and covered myself with it. I was not more than five or ten miles from the dropping point. I lay there and began to wonder about Joan. She may have been caught in that ground barrage. Somewhere there was a hell of a fight going on. I lay there the rest of the night, trying to sleep, hearing the sound of artillery far away.

CHAPTER SEVENTEEN

At dawn I heard a Dornier bomber approaching low and I stuck my head out of the brush pile. The Dornier seemed to lumber across the sky, just above treetop level. I listened to it go away to the south and then the sound of its desynchronized engines returned and it came lumbering back at treetop level. He was looking for something. Certainly not our crew. They wouldn't put a Dornier in the air for that.

When the Dornier was gone I looked out from the brush pile. Forests topped all the hills around, and beyond the plowed field peasants were cutting hay. The air was cold and clear and sunny. Were there Maquis near by or Germans? I still had my pistol and I tested the cylinder and checked the ammo and barrel for dirt. It was clean. In the morning light the sound of bombing and bursts of firing came from across the hills.

I lay there listening to the sound of bombing. It stopped and I listened to the drone of Heinkels going away. Then it was silent. Suddenly into the silence came the sound of walking. The sound was quite near. I wiggled forward a little, out of the brush pile, so I could see clearly into the woods. I peered through the leaves. I thought of my pistol and pulled it out and took the safety catch off and focused my eyes as sharply as possible into the trees. The foliage

118

was thick and I watched the man – a short, stocky man, hatless, in worn battle jacket and frayed trousers. He emerged into an opening and looked around, slanting his head as if listening.

When the man moved I saw that he was drawing a rope along behind him. Attached to the rope was an amputated human leg.

I waited until he passed. Then I followed and called to him. The man stopped quickly. He had a wide peasant face, bearded. He looked surprised, stopping in mid-stride.

I said, 'British. American.' He did not move. The bloody and dirty amputated leg lay in the path.

Suddenly the man smiled and walked toward me. I covered him with the pistol.

'Boom!' he said with a great laugh and gestured with one hand to signify the diving crash of an airplane. He smiled at me.

'Where's headquarters?' I asked. The man thrust out his hand as if to shake hands. I stepped back. He shook his head.

'Hospital,' he said and pointed to the southwest. He shook his head sadly again. 'Burn . . . crash . . .'

'Did you find any of my men?' I asked him. He did not seem to understand. Suddenly I realized I must be at least fifty miles from where the crew had bailed out. And my French was bad.

I pulled the map out of my flying boot. I spread it out on the ground and picked at what I thought was our approximate position. Somewhere near Aurillac. He pointed to our position on the map. I pointed to where the drop was.

'St. Martial,' I said. He shook his head.

'Too many Germans,' he said. 'Big battle.'

'I want to get there,' I said.

He shook his head. I folded the map.

'What about the hospital?' I said. 'Take me there.'

Perhaps from there I could contact Joan somewhere near the drop point. He jerked his head and told me to walk ahead of him. He picked up the rope and began dragging the leg.

I walked down a faintly worn path. The wind slapped the trees. The path seemed to turn upon a circle. He

119

stopped and walked a few yards at right angles to the path and stepped over a fallen tree. From a pack on his back he carefully sprinkled dirt over his tracks to the tree. Then he beckoned me to follow him into the woods. Now and then a burst of gunfire came from across the hills. Twice invisible German aircraft passed overhead and died away. Where we stepped out onto a sandy road the corpse of a peasant was hanging from a tree. We passed it and went on down the road and turned back into the forest.

Behind me the man walked, dragging the rope, pulling the limb like a deer hunter bringing in the kill. The woods ceased. The path rose, curving out of the trees. The man stopped. He looked briefly over his shoulder. From his shoulder pack he again threw dirt on his footprints. He picked up the leg and slung it across his shoulder. It wasn't until later I learned the leg was used to throw the German Alsatian tracking dogs off the trail.

'Come on,' he said sharply.

The sandy road narrowed and the foliage and trees grew thicker and larger and the stones that lined the road were covered with moss. We went on silently for half an hour. The man halted and drew back a small clump of bushes beside the road. He jerked his head and indicated that I was to follow. We went on into the undergrowth. The floor of the forest was stony. The man stopped, turned over one stone. The bottom was bare. He stepped upon the bare side and lifted up the next moss covered stone and told me to follow, using the bare side of the first stone to step on. We walked a hundred yards, turning over moss covered stones and replacing them after stepping on the bare side. During the next mile we did the same thing twice again.

He stopped in front of a clump of weeds and carefully stepped up onto two parallel tree trunks, long and thin. I followed, keeping one foot on each trunk. Then he climbed a ladder of tree trunks built up on rocks that took us to the top of a limestone rock. We crossed the rock on thin, split tree trunks which the man gathered up behind us. We had left no sign, noise or track. I was very hungry. But where the hell am I? I thought.

And then I saw the hollow below, and two log cabins below the surface of the ground, camouflaged by a screen of pines.

I watched a man emerge from one cabin. He was wearing an Allied battle dress jacket and the civilian riding trousers that I understood later were almost a uniform for Maquis officers. He wore English infantry officer's boots and he carried a submachine gun under his right arm. He was bareheaded.

We walked up to him and I saluted.

'Who is he?' he asked angrily of the man who had brought me in.

'RAF,' I said. He nodded and stared at me. I looked at his thin, shaven face. It was a long, lean face. His eyes were wide. He looked as if he had been shot through the face, just under the jaw bone, and the welt of the scar showed jaggedly on each cheek.

'Colonel Baspo,' he said in English. Then he grinned. I liked his looks.

'Can you prove your identity?' he asked.

'Where is the girl I dropped last night?' I asked.

The Maquis colonel studied me for a long moment.

'Where did you drop?'

'St. Martial. I got shot down going back.'

'Fool,' he said angrily in French to the man who had brought me in.

The man shrugged, jabbered something about my gun.

'What is her name?' the colonel asked sullenly.

'Joan DeMarney,' I said. 'She's supposed to be carrying money and orders.'

'Money,' he spat. 'We need guns and ammunition!'

'Where is she?'

'At the front.'

'Can I see her?'

'You can't get through. Perhaps tonight.'

'Why not?'

'The area is infested with Germans. You are on a plateau. The S.S. is all around. Twenty thousand. Every type of support, artillery, mortars.'

'Where is she?'

'At Fridfront. We're going to try to get through tonight.'

'What are your plans?'

'Try to pull out the men at night.'

'Are these your headquarters?'

The colonel nodded and said, 'Headquarters and hospital. Come in.' As we walked toward the cabin a fawn walked toward the colonel. He fed it something from his hand. It was a pet, he said, that they had had for several months. In the first room there were twelve patients, all limb wounds. In the next room were six patients, all head wounds.

'What will you do if the Germans pinch you off?'

'The forest has been our home for four years, We will transfer the patients over the mountains as before. If we can evacuate the brigade from Fridfront we shall have to move the hospital tomorrow night.'

'Do you have anything to eat?'

The idea seemed to amuse him. He grinned, looking at me.

'Are you hungry?' he asked.

'Starved.'

It was the first time I ever ate cold pork and pickled mushrooms and wine for breakfast.

'Why don't they send more bazookas?' the colonel asked.

I grinned at him. 'You'll have to take that up with Joan.'

'They are excellent against troops lying in rocks.'

As we ate, the rattle of Maquis machine guns raced across the morning air. Mortar fire rose in answer.

In the twilight when the planes came I heard the bombs falling and the firing start and my heart seemed to jerk with every sound.

They've probably killed her down there, I thought, listening to the heavy firing. I licked my dry lips. Then the heavy firing stopped and I could hear grenades popping like firecrackers on a Fourth of July evening. A hollow feeling came into my chest.

It wasn't until nine o'clock that night that the colonel said it was time to go. It was dark and I checked the dial of my wrist watch. I said, 'What's the schedule?'

'We'll find a way in.'

'In?' I said. 'How're you going to get them out?'

'That remains to be seen.'

'Haven't you had any contact with—'

'Not since last night,' he said. 'We will take five men. Can you handle a rifle?'

'Machine gun or rifle.'

The S.S. troops held the valley all around the plateau.

The colonel believed also that some had infiltrated between Fridfront and the hospital. We started through the woods and moved along a small stream. The leaves of the trees moved in the night wind. The night was quiet and clear and we came out into a meadow and passed two haycocks and entered the forest again.

Near the edge of the town we were fired on. We lay on the ground until the firing ceased and challenged the position. The colonel shouted, 'Baspo! It is Baspo!' We did not know their password. I heard a rifle bolt snick as it was pulled back. Steep-walled, a building loomed against the night sky. A rifle fired and then another, stabbing the dark with yellow flashes. I pushed my head hard against the ground.

'Don't shoot,' Baspo yelled. 'Don't shoot! We are coming in.'

'Who are you?' a voice called from the ruined wall of the stone building.

'There are seven of us. Goddamn you, it's me! Colonel—'

Before he could finish, the firing of several rifles crashed and crackled along the building.

'Have you a woman with you?' he called. 'Joan! The English courier!'

'Yes, sir,' said a voice, lower now, almost ashamed, as if it had suddenly recognized the colonel's voice.

'Come in one at a time,' another voice said from the ruined building wall.

I could hear them talking behind the wall. Then a voice shouted, 'Listen, you Nazi bastards.' It was an American voice.

'Hey,' I shouted. 'We're not Krauts. I'm the RAF pilot who dropped the woman last night. Is she with you?'

'Don't con me,' said the American voice. 'Here. Give me a grenade, Hubert.'

'Listen,' I said. 'I don't know who you are but we're screwed out here. We're not Nazis. Believe me. Do you know Red Grange?'

'Hey, wait a minute,' said the American voice. 'He's sure got us conned or he is a Yank.'

'No,' the colonel shouted. 'Don't be a fool. We have a radio. Let us come in and we can call London for a drop.'

'You are Baspo?' a French voice called out.

'For Crissake,' the colonel shouted. 'Who the hell are you expecting?'

'Drop your guns and come in with your hands up,' a voice commanded.

'Stand up,' the colonel said. 'Keep your hands up.'

We all rose, dropped our weapons, put our hands up.

'One at a time. Keep your hands up high,' the French voice called.

The colonel walked toward the ruined wall of the building. Other walls seemed to evolve from the shadowy darkness as we approached the edge of the town.

'I can't jump this wall,' the colonel said.

'Don't move your hands,' the French voice ordered.

'I am not a high jumper,' the colonel said.

'Hubert, give me a grenade,' the American voice said.

'Shoot the first one,' another voice said. 'It will show who they are if they return fire.'

'It sounds like the colonel,' another voice said. 'Maybe those are Huns behind him.'

'Shut up, fools,' the colonel shouted. 'I am your commanding officer. You will all die if we don't set up an arms drop for you with this radio.'

'We will all die anyway,' said another voice. 'We might as well ask for music on that radio.'

'Come on. Come on, before you bring the Krauts in with you,' shouted the American voice.

The colonel put one leg up on the ruined window sill of the ruined wall. I saw him pushing himself up.

I heard the snick of a rifle bolt.

'Get that fucking gun down,' the colonel shouted.

'Listen, Mac,' shouted the American voice. 'One wrong move and I'll blow you a new ass hole.'

'Throw it, you dumb bastard,' the colonel yelled. 'Go on, throw it.'

'Ah, let him have it,' another voice said. 'Them Krauts'll work any angle.'

'Look,' the colonel said. He straddled the window sill. He did not move. He looked as if he were ready to duck either way if somebody started firing or bombing. 'You want to kill somebody big. I'm not a colonel. Just a sergeant.' He laughed.

'He's probably right,' one voice said.

'Sure,' the colonel said. He kept one hand by his side, ready to grab his revolver if he were rushed suddenly. 'Why shoot a sergeant when you can get a real colonel later? Besides, the Krauts have you sewed up.'

'Up your jacksee, Mac,' the American voice yelled. 'You aren't fooling us! Keep your hands up!'

The colonel lifted his arms, raising his hands away from the revolver.

I watched the colonel climb through the ruined window and disappear. There was no sound. No voices. No firing. We waited a long few minutes.

'All right, you guys,' the American voice yelled. 'Come on in.'

There were five of us. When we climbed the wall through the ruined window we found the colonel being embraced by an American in a leather jacket and riding breeches.

'I'm sorry,' he said. 'I'm Nelson, with the O.S.S.'

'Who's in charge?' Colonel Baspo asked him. 'Where's Jacques?'

'Dead,' said Nelson. 'The English girl is giving orders.'

'That's right,' a woman's voice said in the darkness. 'Step out here in the light.' It was Joan but I could not see her.

A flashlight shone in our faces, roving fast from one face to the next.

'Hello,' she said curtly to me. 'Colonel, where is the radio?' She flashed the light among us. She walked over to the man with the radio transmitter. 'Can you send?'

'He's slow,' Colonel Baspo said.

'Where did you get him?'

'He has been with us since the Englishman was killed.'

'Hunter?' she asked.

'Yes,' said the colonel. 'Last week.'

'Does he know the code?'

'No. You must write it out for him.'

'All right. Have him prepare to send.'

She shone the flashlight on a piece of paper and, pressing the paper against the wall, she began to write with a pencil.

'Hurry,' she said, handing the message to the man with

the transmitter. She bent over him, shining the light on his machine.

The radio operator stooped busily over the transmitter.

'Come on, come on,' the colonel told him. 'Quickly or we are all cooked.'

The radio operator looked up, smiled slowly. Then his hand became busy at the telegraph key.

'All right,' he said after a few minutes. 'The message is sent.'

'You, Colonel,' Joan said. 'You command now. I know the American. He is the pilot who dropped me.'

The colonel saluted her.

'I will take you to our place,' she said to me. Then to the colonel: 'Do not stay here long. They will shell the town on the hour. We are dug in below, just beyond the town where the hill starts.'

We started along between the ruined walls of the town and in the dark I stumbled over the rubble and shards of masonry. I could smell the dead in the buildings.

Joan stopped suddenly.

'Walk slowly,' she said.

'What's up?'

'The guards shoot almost without speaking. Keep your pistol ready if you have one.' Then I saw she was carrying a Sten gun.

We walked slowly along the rubble-filled street in the dark. Gradually the street began to descend, curving past ruined buildings, and then it gave way to fields and we went on under trees glittering with stars.

CHAPTER EIGHTEEN

The leaves overhead twinkled with starlight. I lay curled in the foxhole and waited for Joan to return. She said she had to go back to see the colonel again to ask for ten men to help her handle the drop and to be sure he set the time and place with each man. My hands felt cold and my legs tired and a deadly tension I could not throw off still seemed to grip my spine. Suddenly the darkness seemed to rock crazily. The air around me seemed to swell, roar and thunder. I flattened my body in the foxhole. A cloud of flame shot past. There was an explosion and I felt the ground rise slowly. Then more shells hissed past overhead.

'Take cover,' I heard voices shouting in the darkness. The air heaved again. Flames lit up the darkness. Clods of earth rained down upon my back. I wiped the dirt out of my eyes. Shells whistled over again. I clawed myself against the ground. I felt someone leap in beside me. I turned, felt in the darkness. It was Joan. High explosives crashed against the hillside. I could hardly breathe. My lungs seemed to tighten with each shell burst. My head began to feel swollen and I thought I was suffocating.

Just as suddenly as it started the shelling ceased.

She laughed. 'Piece of cake?'

'I'll stick to flying.'

I felt suddenly ashamed and idiotic. I had never experienced a bombardment like this. It was worse than being twenty thousand feet in the sky under heavy flak fire. But she did not seem unnerved in the least.

She curled her body against mine, fitting the length of her breasts and stomach and legs against my back, jack-knifing her knees to fit against the back of my legs and knees. She kissed my neck.

'Not quite the Berkeley,' she said. I rolled over and kissed her.

'Room service?'

'Your order, please, sir.'

I held her closer and she pressed her hair against my cheek.

'Oh, darling, I love you and I heard the plane had been shot down.'

'If we get out of this I'm getting you fired,' I said.

'If they don't drop tomorrow we aren't getting out of it. They're almost out of ammunition.'

'Didn't he get through to London?' I asked.

'No,' she said.

'Well, we've always had a lot of luck.'

'We'd better sleep.'

'It'll be dawn soon.'

'There's still time to sleep,' she said. 'You'll need it tomorrow.'

'What's the real picture?'

'We should be able to fall back in another day.'

'What makes you think so?'

'We aren't surrounded yet.'

'What do you call it?'

'Some men are coming up from the south.'

'What happened to the radio?'

'There isn't enough power to transmit.'

I wish I knew what was going to happen to us, I thought. I had never completely given up in any tight spot, but if the Germans shut us off from behind they could finish us off in no time.

'Can you fire a rifle or machine gun?' she asked.

'Sure.'

'We will bring one in here tomorrow.'

'Where's the rest of the line?'

'You're in it,' she said. 'We're dug in on the slope. Tomorrow we'll move into one of the dugouts. I don't like to move around in the dark. We're apt to draw our own fire.'

She grinned. 'Let's sleep.'

In the darkness she curled against me and we held each other tight. But it was a long time before I slept.

In the morning we woke on the side of the mountain with the town behind us on the high plateau. A damp mist moved up the side of the mountain and we watched an air battle going on above the valley. A Messerschmitt 109 plunged down in flames out of the sunlight. Cheers rose from the foxholes all along the slope. All day the valley muttered with machine-gun fire and trench mortars but the Germans did not attack. That night as soon as it was dark the colonel came along the line and told us we were to withdraw in an hour. We walked through the ruined town. On the road in the valley below, trucks and cars were waiting. We drove a line of cars and trucks through the darkness into a pass between more mountains. The trucks stopped after an hour.

'Out!' the colonel shouted, sending the order down the column. 'Up the mountains.'

We walked in single file. Joan walked ahead. The slope rose more steeply.

'Got the grenades and stick bombs?' Nelson, the O.S.S. officer, asked.

'All set,' answered the man named Hubert.

We went on up the mountain. The colonel called the column to a halt. 'We'll hold the road. That will stop them from coming through the pass or flanking us.' His voice was quite loud, very clear in the darkness. High above the moon hung naked and white. In the moonlight we could see the road below.

'They'll never get up that road,' Joan said.

'Dig in here,' the colonel said. On the horizon we could hear the thundering of the rear-guard action in the town. I listened to the sound of artillery and the exploding shells.

We lay on the ground, feeling the stones digging into our sides.

The moon shone brighter and brighter as the night went on. After a while clouds scudded across the sky.

It began to rain lightly. The morning rose gray and misty. I listened to the roaring shells across the top of the mountain.

'Long range guns,' Joan said. It was still raining.

When daylight came the shelling ceased.

'Cloutier and Montieth, you bring up the dynamite,' the colonel shouted. The column rose and we began climbing the mountain. It went on raining. A man stood on the skyline waving his arms.

Just below the crest of the mountain we found that positions had been prepared. Joan and I crawled into a dugout. It was small and narrow, blown out of rock. We sat with our knees drawn up and watched the road far below and the column of men climbing the side of the mountain.

'A bit small in here,' I said.

'It'll keep us that much warmer.' She called down the mountain to one of the men bringing up railroad ties. He was leading a mule. He unloaded the ties in front of our dugout. When the rain stopped we pulled the heavy ties over the hole. Nelson came past from the colonel's command post below on the reverse side of the mountain.

'They'll be on us in the morning,' he said.

'Any machine guns?' I asked. 'I can handle one.'

'I'll see,' Nelson said and went away. I rearranged the railroad ties across the front of our dugout.

They did not look firm and substantial.

'Come on,' Joan said. 'We'll pile rocks on them.' When we finished Nelson returned with a machine gun. It was an old-fashioned Vickers gas-operated pan-fed .303, set on a small metal tripod. We set it up with a good field of fire. We lay back against the rock. We were exhausted.

'God's teeth,' Joan said. 'I can't feel a thing.'

Slowly the sun died and the twilight rose greenly from the valley. The moon rose in the sky and the air became bright and still. There was no sound, only a profound, empty silence.

'Goblin's night,' I said.

'They won't attack until tomorrow.'

'What's the point in trying to hold out here with so few men?' I asked. She did not answer. I listened to a stone bouncing down the slope of the mountain.

'The hospitals,' she said. 'We have to hold out until they move the wounded further south. The Germans kill everybody in a field hospital.'

'You get some sleep.'

She lay back. I put a pan of ammo on the gun and cocked it and squatted and looked down the mountain. Far below I heard a motorcycle moving. In the darkness I saw a figure approach. It was Hubert. He leaned across the barricade.

'We thought we'd lost you,' he said.

'What's up?'

'The Germans have passed through the town,' he said.

'How long ago?'

'Three hours.'

'Anything else?'

'Fresh troops. Paratroopers.'

'The S.S. aren't enough?'

He grinned. 'Watch yourself,' he said. 'Don't fall asleep.'

He went on to the next dugout. I watched him stoop and crawl and disappear over the top of the ridge. The moon waxed palely.

I cocked and recocked the machine gun again. I did not trust it. It was too old. I had not seen a Vicker gas-operated pan-model since early flying school. I remembered that their rate of fire was very slow and, nine times out of ten, if you got a stoppage you had to take the pan

130

off. The cartridge was always slipping incorrectly off the pan into the feed.

Hubert came back, this time coming directly over the top of our dugout and jumping down in front of us.

'We need a railroad tie for the anti-tank gun emplacement,' he said.

'You won't get it here,' I said.

'I've got orders.'

'How the hell is a tank going to come up that rocky open slope?'

'I want one of your ties.'

'Get the hell out of here,' I said, lifting the machine gun.

He cursed and went off. I watched him moving along the slope, descending. He stopped two dugouts below us. Again he must have been refused. Of course, everybody figured he was only trying to get an extra tie for his own dugout. He came back to the dugout next to ours.

One of the riflemen stuck his head out. 'You don't get it here.' He pointed a rifle at Hubert.

'Colonel's orders!'

'Get it in writing,' the rifleman said.

'While the tanks are blowing you out?'

'We're screwed anyway,' said the rifleman.

Hubert went off. The two Maquis riflemen called to us and I went over. They had two canteens of brandy and offered us a drink. I took one canteen back and we drank and listened to the sound of aircraft engines coming low through the valley. They sounded like Heinkels. They passed on the far side of the opposite mountain. From far away came the thunder of heavy artillery.

'Here come the fireworks,' Joan said.

We listened to the firing and heard the shells exploding on the far side of the opposite mountain.

'Hey,' yelled a voice from the next dugout. 'Don't drink all the cognac.'

CHAPTER NINETEEN

Maquis with rifles slung across their shoulders lay on the rocks in front of our dugout. In the morning light they looked dirty and desperate, their eyes and faces strained. Below them a short line of Maquisards with rifles slung over their shoulders came plodding up the side of the mountain. They were Spanish. They carried satchels of TNT.

'They're bringing up flame-throwers,' said one of the Maquis in front of our dugout.

'Were you in the rear guard?' I asked.

'Christ,' he said and shook his head.

'Have they been reinforced?'

'Mortars. Spotter aircraft. More artillery.'

I climbed out of the dugout and sat on the ground with them.

'They'll burn us out here too,' he said. 'They burned us out of the town.'

'You held them a long time.'

'Shit,' he said and spat.

The Maquisards, wearing Spanish caps, passed by, the TNT satchels slung on their backs. Joan said they were experts at blowing up bridges, having practiced considerably during the Spanish Civil War.

A single German fighter flew over, fast and low, upon us suddenly before we heard the sound of his engine. One Maquis rifleman dived into our dugout and jammed himself between Joan and myself. 'Christ,' he muttered. 'Why can't we get an air drop?'

'It's coming,' Joan lied.

'It better or we're cooked.'

The sound of machine-gun fire from the German fighter came from the reverse side of the mountain.

'Let's dig in,' said the Maquis to his comrades and climbed out of our dugout. 'Those bastards'll be back with bombs.' They rose wearily and climbed to the crest of the ridge and vanished below. Others came up the side of the

132

mountain. All carried rifles but they looked exhausted, staring out of numbed faces covered with dust.

Two anti-tank gun crews came over the crest of the ridge and slowly descended. I watched them getting into position in a hollow at the base of the mountain.

Where are the Krauts? I thought. It was too quiet. There was no sound.

Suddenly a cloud of white smoke burst directly above us. I crouched behind the gun. A string of white smoke balls burst below.

'What the hell is that?' I said.

'Range,' Joan said. I felt her beside me. She sounded very placid. I glanced at her face. She was staring out steadily, her eyes and face quite calm, almost serene.

Another string of white puffs, like magical blossoms, burst in a long string above the slope. Earth rose in a black fountain far down the slope of the mountain.

The Maquis rifleman came over from the next dugout. He was whistling to himself. He sat out in front of our dugout.

I've got to get Joan out of here, I thought.

A gust of smoke hung above the base of the mountain, faded, and another filled the air. Somewhere a machine gun began to hammer and the ground began to reverberate from exploding shells.

'They're getting the range,' Joan said.

The Maquis rifleman stopped whistling abruptly. I heard machine guns hammering far away. Then I heard a noise like the rush of an express train. There was a boom and a sharp crack and just below us a fountain of earth rose out of a plume of black smoke. Then the rushing, roaring, swishing, booming sound came again and dirt fountained again.

The Maquis rifleman rose like a running dog in full stride and vanished headfirst into his dugout. The earth spouted black and gray geysers below us.

I caught Joan's arm.

'Get down behind these ties,' I said. 'I'm going to see Colonel Baspo.'

'What?' she asked in the roar of another explosion.

I jumped out of the dugout.

'Baspo!' I shouted back. There was nobody visible. I

ran up the mountain to the crest and plunged down the reverse slope. Below was a large dugout. I saw Colonel Baspo standing in front talking to one of the Maquisards. Suddenly the shelling ceased. The air was deathly still.

'What do you want?' Baspo's face was red and swollen.

'I want to get the girl out of here.'

'You can't.'

'She'll do more good for your cause if you get her out.'

'She knows how to shoot. We've had her with us before.' He smiled. 'They can't get up the hill without tanks and tanks can't do it.'

'It's a nice theory,' I said.

'Come on,' he smiled. 'I'll show you.'

We walked to the crest of the mountain. He handed me his field glasses and began to talk in terms of fields of fire, how the Germans could not advance up such a slope of rock without tanks and tanks could not traverse such an open field of fire.

I looked at the ridge of the mountain across the valley. I heard the fire of forty-millimeter guns.

'Look,' I said, handing him the field glasses. 'They're starting down toward the road.'

Artillery opened up again.

'It's a nice theory,' I said and walked away.

'Are you crazy?' Joan said when I got back. 'You could have been hit.'

'Baspo is crazy.'

'He knows what he's doing.'

'The pride of St. Cyr.'

Geysers of dirt spouted all along the road below. We crouched in our dugout, close to each other. Explosions hammered against our ears. The air felt as if it were splitting apart. Dirt and pieces of volcanic rock fell all around us. The earth seemed to roll and lurch in the whistling, screaming sound of shells exploding. One of the Maquis riflemen from the next dugout crawled over.

'They've knocked out our artillery!'

I felt fear roll up in waves through my stomach.

'They want the machine guns down below,' he said.

'This old crock?'

'Come on,' he said. 'They'll put the infantry in soon.'

134

'Stay here,' I said to Joan. She did not appear to hear me. She picked up the extra pans of ammo.

'Come on. Come on,' she said in a tight voice. 'Let's go! Let's go!'

I took the machine gun and we crawled down the slope. We inched our way along between shell bursts, ducking behind rocks.

'Jesus, Jesus, Jesus,' the rifleman kept saying whenever the barrage lifted. I listened to the shells bursting high on the ridge. I began to pant. I could hear Joan breathing heavily.

'Baspo is insane,' said the rifleman.

'Absolutely,' I said.

We crawled on. I heard shells passing overhead and saw them bursting on the side of the mountain beyond the road.

We reached another dugout in a string of dugouts that stretched across the lower half of the mountain slope. We entered a big dugout.

'Everybody's shot to hell,' said Nelson, the O.S.S. officer.

An old empty feeling filled me. My legs and arms and body felt dull and dead. Come on, come on, I thought.

'All right,' Nelson said. 'Everybody out. You, Joan and you—' he looked at me— 'give us covering fire. We're going to counterattack across the road. They're bringing up flamethrowers.'

My God, I thought, looking at the ten men in the dugout. Counterattack?

'Out!' Nelson shouted. The men went out without speaking. I set up the gun. I suddenly felt like laughing. It seemed somehow ridiculously ironic that we were safe here and these men were going down the slope to certain death. Lying flat on my belly and looking down the slope I watched them go. I steadied the gun and fired a burst over their heads into the trees across the road. Machine-gun fire hammered from the mountainside across the road.

'They're going to attack across the open,' Joan said.

I did not say anything. I was suddenly not so afraid to die as I was angry at being caught with her in such a trap. I could joke about it but I hated the thought of dying now more than ever before in the war. And I was angry. Why

135

must she die? Why in hell must she die? I hated every second of it.

Geysers of black earth leaped up along the base of the mountain. I watched the line of men advance. The artillery ceased for a lone minute, then started up again. It sounded heavier.

'Eighty-eights,' Joan said.

'They're across the road!' I fired short bursts, fast, into the trees across the road, lifting the fire.

Suddenly the mountain rolled under us. Dust and stones struck us in the face and upon the shoulders and arms. I grabbed Joan and dragged her into the deepest corner of the dugout and pressed her against the wall and held her there.

'They don't like your machine gun,' she said.

Suddenly the shelling ceased. Suddenly there was no sound. I looked down into the empty valley. From the grove of trees across the road came the chatter of machine-gun fire.

'Well, they got that far,' Joan said.

I could hear German machine pistols firing and then it was quiet.

Suddenly there was a deep bark and roar of an eighty-eight. I fired a long burst high into the trees across the road. Shells burst over our heads almost immediately.

A Messerschmitt fighter-bomber flew low along the road, machine-gunning the ditch. I could not hear any fire from the Maquis across the road. Twilight came slowly up through the trees, up through the valley, rising like green water, mounting steadily up the slope.

'Are you hungry?' Joan asked.

'Starved. I'll see what I can scrounge.'

I crawled out of the dugout and up the side of the mountain to the ridge. Down below Hubert was passing out food next to the colonel's dugout. Bread and cheese and wine.

'Only one ration,' he said as I reached for two.

'But what about Joan?' I said.

'Is she alive?'

'Of course.'

Hubert handed me bread and cheese and a bottle of wine.

'We can't spare rations,' he said. I started back up the hill with two Maquis riflemen. They walked behind me.

'Keep down on the skyline,' one said.

We went on silently. I listened to them panting. They were carrying both rations and ammunition. We crawled down toward our dugouts. Shells began falling along the side of the mountain and then shrapnel began bursting in black puffs overhead.

'Down!' one Maquis shouted. The shell bursts flashed in the darkening air, exploding on the reverse slope. I got up and began to run.

Joan was leaning against the machine gun.

'What happened to the bread?' she said.

'My God,' I said. 'I must have dropped it.' I ran back up the slope.

'Jack!' she yelled. 'Jack!'

The shells went over, bursting below. I scoured the path down which we had come. I could not find the bread. I ran back to the dugout.

'You made a nice target of yourself on that ridge,' she said.

'They must have picked it up,' I said.

The two Maquis in the next dugout crept over.

'Here are some grenades they sent down,' one said.

'Thank you very much,' Joan said.

CHAPTER TWENTY

Joan and I watched out through the front of the dugout. We had three grenades each and we put them on the ground beside the machine gun.

The night was dark and silent and then the tracer firing began, red and green threads of fire, lancing across the valley.

Somewhere an eighty-eight fired and into the roar came the sound of machine pistols firing rapidly in long bursts.

Down on the road somebody began to scream and moan. The screams rose and died away in the bellowing of heavy guns. The moon came up slowly over the mountain.

The tracer firing laced the darkness.

137

'Bastille Day,' Joan said.

'You better get some sleep,' I said. 'Lie back and shut your eyes anyway.'

The screams and cries of wounded rose across the valley. I felt drowsy. I could feel my head nodding. My eyes wanting to close, closing slowly, then forcing them open. Then I slept. A voice, a hand, roused me. I grabbed for the machine gun. A figure loomed in the dugout entrance.

'Hey, take it easy,' said a voice. It was Nelson the O.S.S. officer.

'What happened?' I asked.

'Dead,' he said. 'All dead.'

'It was a foolish attack.'

'Had to. Tank in the trees.'

'Did you get it?'

'Yes,' he said. 'Christ. Have you got a drink?'

I handed him the half-empty bottle of wine. He drank and sat with his knees pulled up against his chest. Then he said, 'Christ, they promised us some artillery cover when we crossed the road. There was nothing! The tank caught us in the open. Just on the edge of the trees. We crawled around behind it just before dark and had a line on it only they've got mortars on top of the mountain and they put fire down on their own position. They knocked out the tank themselves and kept us pinned down and then brought up a heavy and started shelling us. I got up and ran. There wasn't anything you could do. Lie there and get blown to hell or run and get cut down.'

His voice ceased. He drank again, tilting his head, the wine running out of the corners of his mouth, down his neck.

'I crawled damn near all the way back up here. Both the anti-tank guns in the grove are knocked out. Crews and all. Why in hell can't we get some support?'

The moon rose higher, round and naked and white. He thanked us for the wine and got up and went on up toward the ridge.

It was just before dawn when the first heavy barrage began. There were more guns firing now.

'Here it comes,' Joan said. We got down behind the ties. The shell bursts rolled up the mountainside, creeping steadily, went over the ridge and stopped.

138

A small German observation plane flew over, circled our position and flew back toward the east.

'Here they go again,' Joan said. Her face was white and chalky. The ground began to shake. I felt my hands shaking. Clouds of flame shot up ahead of us. The barrage roared, thundered.

A rail tie broken in two pieces sailed past the front of the dugout. The shells passing overhead made a hissing sound.

'They've brought up a lot of heavies,' Joan said nervously. The gray dawn light split into pieces of fire. The rock seemed to heave under us. Explosions lit up the slope.

There was not going to be any escape this time. Through a crack between the ties I watched the slope surge and heave in fountains of flames.

Rocks flew about like shrapnel. Rocks rained down upon the dugout. A hot shocking blow struck my left shoulder. I did not feel anything. I reached to touch it and something struck my head. I felt my body sliding away from me. I held hard to the machine-gun butt. I shook my head, felt my shoulder. It was only numb, no blood, no pain.

Someone began firing a machine-gun on our left. My head boomed and roared with concussion. Through the gray light came more flashing of fire from heavy explosions. Hollow, furious blasts.

The two Maquis came over from the next dugout. Their dugout had almost been destroyed. There was barely room in ours for them but we squeezed in.

'They'll attack soon,' one Maquis said. 'When the barrage lifts.'

Suddenly the shelling ceased. From the grove across the road, figures in steel German helmets emerged and started up the slope. Machine guns barked from above and below us.

The rocky slope was cratered, torn. I watched the first wave of Germans advance, running. Rifle and machine-gun fire poured down on them. Men fell but the line climbed steadily, taking cover, advancing.

The two Maquis had a box of grenades and they began rolling them down the hill, one hundred yards and further. Another line of smooth-helmeted figures emerged from

139

the grove and started up the hill. The first wave had about fifty per cent casualties. I watched them carefully, holding fire until they were closer, estimating the range.

Now I saw their faces, grimacing, contorted. I began firing. The gun stopped. I cleared the stoppage. A face reared in front, fell away, distorted. The gun hammered against my shoulder. Figures whirled, vanished. Joan went on pitching grenades.

I felt overwhelmed with a viciousness and ferocity. The barrel was hot and I changed pans of ammunition. I had a murderous desire to keep firing into the dead bodies on the slope.

By noon the sun was blazing. The attack had failed. The broken line of helmeted figures retreated across the road. I watched them bring up mortars. I lay back exhausted.

The rocky slope, barren, cratered as the moon, lay blasted, silent and empty. I looked at Joan. I had lost all feeling for her. I felt dead. I lay back panting. She lay against me, unable to speak. One of the Maquis lay dead against the wall, the top of his head blown off.

We lay in the dugout all afternoon, not moving, hardly speaking. The barrage went on, raking the mountain. Smoke and dust filled the dugout. Even the rocks smelled scorched outside.

The young Maquis began to whimper.

'Get your friend out,' I said.

He stared at me blankly. I grabbed the dead man's ankles, dragged him over the ties and dropped him below on the rock.

'We should surrender,' said the Maquis. I looked at him. His lips were trembling. In the fading sky, a parachute flare rose. The shelling diminished.

'I'm going to get some grub,' I said. The Maquis stared glassy-eyed down into the valley.

'Come on,' I said, shaking his arm.

'No,' he mumbled and began to whimper. I climbed out over the ties and twisted and dodged up the mountain. It was dark now. The shelling had stopped.

'Baspo is dead,' Nelson said.

'What happened?'

'Direct hit.'

'Any food?'

'We're trying to rustle up something.' I sat against the ruined dugout. The colonel's body, with both arms gone, lay on its face.

'Where are you going for it?'

'Hubert's gone across country. About two miles.'

Shells burst suddenly all around us. Fragments of rock splattered against my face like bird shot.

We ran down the slope and lay flat. Hubert came up beside us.

'Any luck?' Nelson asked.

'I need three men.'

'What for?'

'Meat. Three dead cows out there in the pasture.'

'You can't go in there until it's dark,' Nelson said. 'The whole pasture is zeroed in.'

We sat and waited. When the moon was out, bright and clear, we went down the reverse slope into the pasture.

'Ha!' Nelson said. The carcasses smelled. 'Aged beef!' We dragged one cow to the corner of the field. Hubert began to butcher it with a trench knife. Suddenly heavy shells howled down upon us. The darkness went mad. The meadow began to burn. We ran across the pasture and up the slope. I went down and crawled into our dugout.

'Oh, God,' Joan said. 'I thought you were dead.'

The Maquis rifleman slept, snoring. Shells began to fall. We crouched under the heavy railroad ties.

'When this lifts,' I said, 'we're getting out of here.'

Toward dawn the shell fire ceased. I lifted her up and out of the dugout. I put one arm around her shoulders and supported her. We began to climb the slope.

I looked back down the slope, across the road. Gray light, the color of muddy water, was rising in the valley. Joan slumped suddenly against me. Her arm was smashed and she fell against me, moaning. I laid her down and took off my shirt and bandaged her arm. The bone showed in the wound. She groaned desperately.

'We aren't far from the hospital,' I said. I tried to comfort her.

Through the bandage the bloodstain widened. I lifted her up on my back. I started up, carrying her, climbing the mountain slowly. *For God's sake, where is the hospital? Have they moved it yet?*

I stopped because the mountainside steepened. I took a deep breath. She cried out with pain. I felt her body shake with the suffering. I heard myself panting. I felt my face and chest swelling under the weight and the climb. I had to get over the ridge fast.

'I'm going to run. It's going to hurt.'

'Go on.'

'All set?'

I shifted her weight on my back. Her smashed arm dangled against my hip. I held her legs tight around my waist and bent forward.

Just as I reached the ridge the barrage began again. Shells hissed overhead. I tried to run, but I almost fell up on the reverse slope. The shell fire increased. I put her down in an abandoned dugout, almost roofless.

'Don't worry,' I said. 'The hospital isn't far from here.'

She did not speak. Then: 'Please find me a drink, darling. Please.'

'Nelson will have one.'

She nodded. A wave of fear rushed over me. *What if the hospital no longer exists? What if the Germans have found it?*

'Joan, does it hurt badly?'

She smiled weakly. 'It won't pull any more parachute rings.'

'Lucky it didn't hit the elbow.'

'Let's find that drink, darling.'

Suddenly her eyes rolled whitely and her face paled.

I got up, lifted her onto my back, and walked slowly.

I began to feel faint, lightheaded. I staggered down to the ruined dugout where Baspo had been killed. My body was shaking. I eased her down on the ground. My head whirled. Nelson handed me a wine bottle filled with water. I knelt down and put my hand under her neck and lifted her head.

I saw Nelson's hand remove the water bottle from my hand. I looked up at him.

'Don't waste it,' he said. 'She's dead.'

I stared at him. 'Her arm is smashed,' I said.

Motionless, Nelson looked down at me. 'Sure, but she's dead.'

'No,' I said. 'She just passed out. Give her some water. She'll be all right.'

Nelson shook his head. 'See for yourself.'

I could not seem to move. My eyes were filled with sweat. 'She's hit in the arm,' I said. 'Give me that water.'

I felt myself rise. I heard my voice. 'Damn you, give me that water! She needs a drink!'

I started toward Nelson. A pistol appeared in his hand.

'Take it easy,' he said, not taking his eyes off me. 'Look at her right side.' I stared down at the small brown stain on the front of her tunic.

'Give me that water!' I heard my voice saying.

Nelson ignored me. He knelt down, slowly rolled Joan over. A single neat hole showed on the right side of her back. Through the liver. She made no sound.

I could not seem to move.

'She was the girl on your drop, wasn't she?'

I nodded. He looked at me, puzzled.

'Did you know her well?'

'No, just on the drop. That's all,' I heard my voice.

I could not seem to move. I looked up at the sky. The high sky shimmered. It was sun-filled now, vivid, shining like glass. And she was dead. The sun seemed to sink. A light wind passed, touching her hair.

EPILOGUE

It is summer now. I feel quiet. The talk I hear seems to be the talk of long ago. Peace. War. And everybody waiting. Is it all only another illusion, a dream from which we never wake? It is almost fifteen years since those days. There is still something burned out in me from those days. Yes, I have adapted myself, nine-till-five, the office desk, and the years have passed.

Here the trees are green with summer again and the cars roll smoothly along the hot summer streets, and in the summer twilight the air, green and soft, is like an old benediction of a time long ago, and the twilight seems to hold a secret we will never know.

On a night like this I am often alone with my thoughts.

The children are away at camp. My wife is at a club meeting. And the memories in those thoughts turn to another time.

The corner street light blooms against the soft summer darkness. I see a picture, an English evening. I am driving into London, along the Great North Road, through Hampstead Heath. The streets are quiet, empty. The buildings of London emerge in the twilight and I remember again what it was like when I was young, experiencing the feelings of love.

The picture seems real, almost upon me. It fades into the light of the street lamp. Along our street stands a line of old elms and now they seem to draw me toward them, the heavy green leafiness of their boughs in the darkness. They are the trees now it seems in the fields beyond the airfield and my heart pauses as I see them moving now in the evening breeze.

When I think like this, alone, a great calmness comes over me. The trees loom like silent apparitions, somehow speaking to me in the wind of time, until a stillness within the night seems to hold suddenly an old and unattainable happiness.

But in the darkness, as the dark leaves turn against the street light, a strange melancholy makes the night almost unbearable for an instant.

A powerful remembrance moves inside me but if I move it will be lost, a mysterious reflection, drawing me back in time, but it is all a dream, an old desire, and I know it.

But even if the dream were to become a reality again, it is too late, because I myself know the tender influences of those hours will never arise in me again.

I turn out the porch light. I feel suddenly like an old traveler. I know only the necessities of life. That is all. The crudities, the superficialities. Yes, and yet I shall not forget the privilege of being a youth in the long, long stream of eternity.